I0771320

POA
R. N. ARCADIA

DEDICATION

This book is dedicated to all the spooky, morbid bitches. Stay wild. Stay weird.

"I was never really insane except upon occasions when my heart was touched."
—EDGAR ALLAN POE

AUTHOR NOTE

Hello *Preylings*!

A few things first.

This is a standalone. A project carefully crafted from my love of Edgar Allan Poe; the daddy of Spook, or one of the originals, anyway. The characters/places/references are symbolic with their names and anagrams. I wanted to switch it up. What if a character was similar to Poe, but was a woman? If you find yourself admiring Poe too, you'll quickly figure out my little clever details hidden throughout this book. I'm cheesy lemon-squeezy; *I apologize for nothing.*

As homage to the man himself, Poa is morbid and is not suited for all readers, and bits of it can be considered taboo and uncomfortable—especially on topics of death and the care of the dead.

Poa is for audiences of age 18+ due to the mature and dark content this book contains.

Some, but not all, content warnings are: Death of family members, death of parents (off-page, or mentioned), death of a bunny (from hunting), suicide, mentions of murder, disturbing scenes with dead bodies in relation to funeral directing, voyeurism, exhibitionism, stalking, slight breath play, hidden/secret identity, suicidal ideation, struggles with mental health, panic attack/anxiety, depression, death aftermath, necromania, grave digging, grave robbing, foster sibling sexual relations.

If I forgot any content themes, it was not my intention. Please read with caution.

All 'quotes in here' are quotes from Edgar Allan Poe himself, who was the inspiration for this story since it's 'darkness and nothing more.'

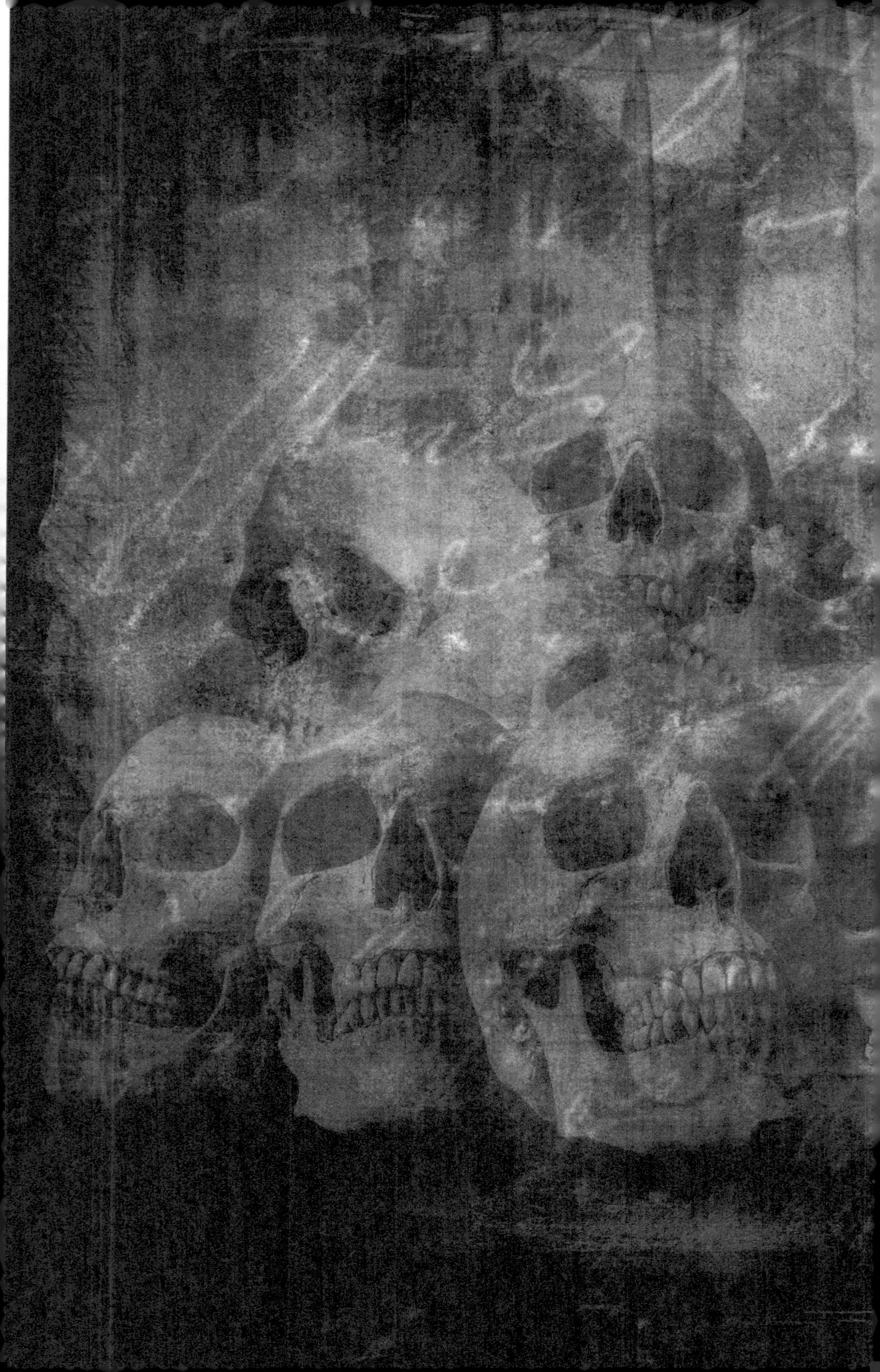

DEATH

The time has come
Misery undone
It is me left standing,
I am the only one

Ghostly echoes have long past
Goodness and life do not last
Light and dark, my only contrast

God, do you hear me?
For all the things that will no longer be
Please place me under the great willow tree

Mourn me not
For all of us will eventually rot
Possessions in the afterlife cannot be brought

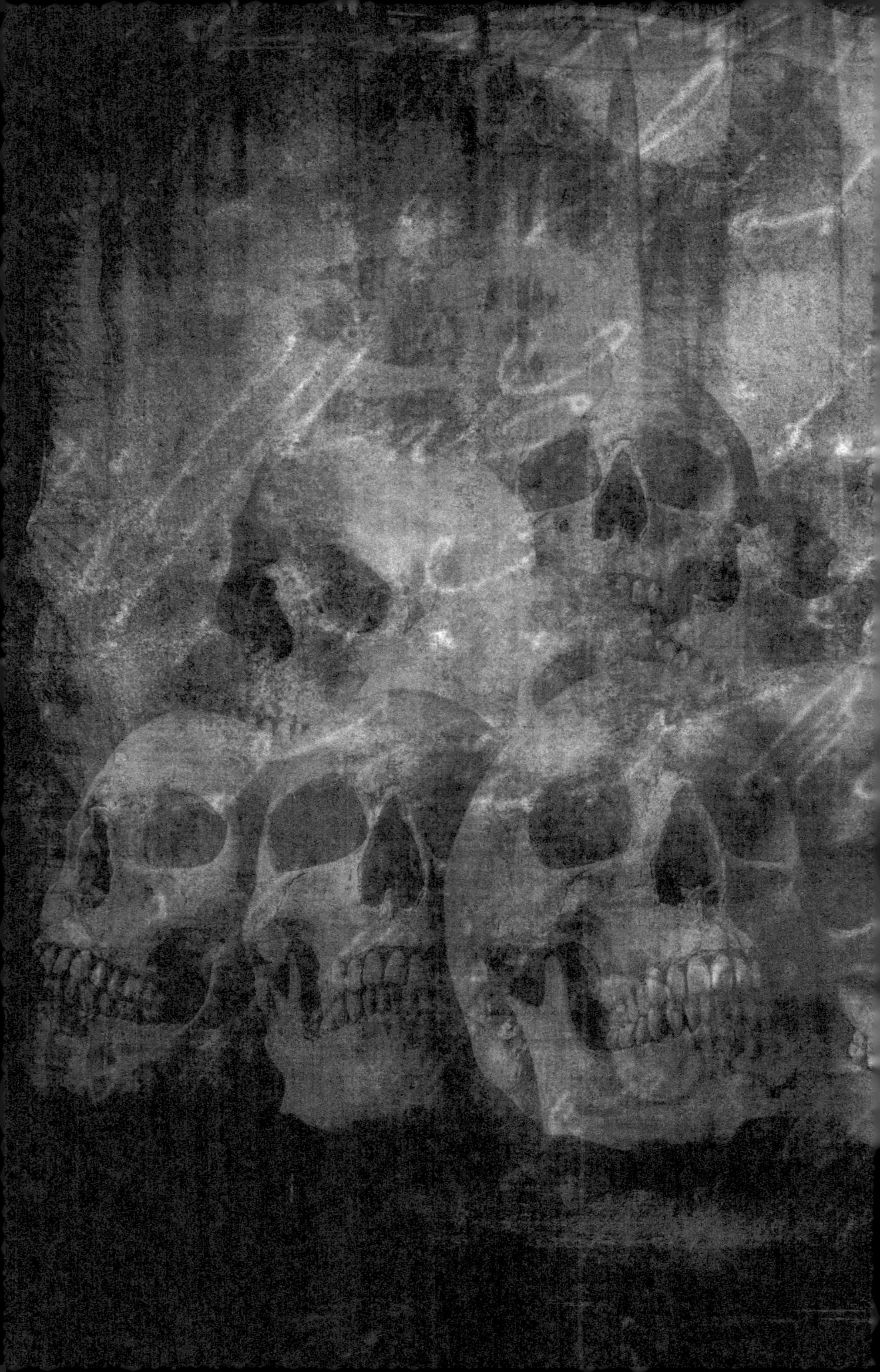

It is a journey, woe or foe
    Covered and buried head to toe
    As above, and so below

Dirt and grime will become in time
    All my memories cannot rewind
    I am sorry to leave you behind

Do not miss me when I am gone
    Only to the reaper, we are pawns
    The stars will still move on, even at dawn

The clock is ticking now
    Grief, I cannot show you how
    What becomes after me, only you allow

No longer can I pretend
    Goodbye, my friend
    For it is me, this is my end

— E.G. Poa

E.G.POA

CHAPTER ONE

THE GRAY

ARDELLA — *Past*

Most people shy away from death.

Not me.

The fascination with it began when I was young. It was a hunter's kill.

My father and older brother had taken me into the woods, showing me how to handle different weapons: knives, guns, a bow and arrow.

The cold steel of the gun was firm in my hands. My father spoke clearly into my ear, *"Hold it at an angle,"* and my grip tightened. *"Remember the kickback."*

I steadied my breathing and kept my eye on the target.

"Squeeze the trigger."

My eyes were glued to the brown rabbit a short distance away, and when my father told me to pull the trigger, I barely registered the bullet leaving the chamber and the kickback as my ears rang loudly from the sound.

Reynolds clapped from three feet away while my father gave me a light tap on the shoulder.

My body thrummed with newfound energy, sizzling my nerves as I stared at the now-emptied space before me, drawing closer to the rabbit that was no longer alive to graze the greenery. There was an initial guilt for taking a life, but then there was a switch in my brain that turned to fascination as I kneeled beside the animal. The oozing wound was the only life left in its tiny body.

"I'm sorry." My voice was barely a whisper as I uttered the words out before tears pooled in my eyes.

Emotions I couldn't quite understand filled me: fascination, guilt, and the finality of what death meant when somebody took it.

Questions swamped my mind. Why was it necessary to hunt and kill? Do animals have souls like us humans? Just what lay beyond that last breath? Was it a deity of light, proclaiming the name of God, the creator of everything, or was it a devil in the underworld with flames and darkness?

Maybe there was an in-between place for people like me who didn't know. A place that wasn't necessarily good or bad. Certainly, there was a balance in the universe between the light and the dark.

The *gray*.

So, there I was, watching the rabbit take its last breath and go still before me, all the questions still swirling in my mind.

The world around me shifted. I stopped hearing the birds and rustling of the leaves. It was me and a dead rabbit. I knew deep within me at that moment that I would never take another life again. Yet, I needed to honor the creature before me somehow.

A gentle hand on my shoulder pulled me out of the foggy sadness that was overcoming me.

"What lives also dies." My father's voice filled my ears, replacing the ringing of the gun's earlier echo.

"Can we bury it?" I asked, wiping my face as he carefully scooped up its lifeless form.

It was just breathing and living, and then there was *nothing*. *I* caused its death. Unnecessarily, all because of my curiosity to experience hunting. I didn't want to play with dolls like my sister, Mackenzie.

"Of course, Ella." His comforting voice eased the tension in my shoulders as we stood in unison.

I followed after him, lost in a trance, focusing only on the little brown limp form he carried.

"Dig a little hole for it, Reyn," I vaguely heard him say once we had stopped. The words sounded muffled as all thoughts emptied from my mind.

Reynolds said nothing, nodding in understanding to our father and using his hands to dig a shallow grave.

"No matter the cause," my father said quietly to me, kneeling to lay the tiny creature in the hole, "you must honor the living and the dead. Luckily, it seems I don't have to teach you that."

He turned to look up at me with a small smile.

Reyn swept the dirt back over the rabbit's dead body until there was nothing left to see. Like it never existed but was only a mere memory.

Was it even real?

"Sometimes, a prayer can be said," my father added, "or you can leave a memento representing life lived. That changes with cultures, but you should do what feels meaningful to you, Ardella."

I caught his pale blue eyes with the slightest wrinkle at the edge of his brow.

"Would you like to say some words?" Reyn asked me, dusting off his hands as he stood.

I nodded in agreement, sniffling.

"I'm sorry, little rabbit. I shall honor you by not taking another life ever again. Sorry for interrupting your lunch."

I bent down to pluck some weeds and placed them over the dirt with a random stick at the top. Wiping my tears, I felt my father stand at my side and hug me with one arm as I stared at what I left behind.

"There. Now, it can rest in peace," my father murmured, kissing the top of my head.

Would it truly rest in peace?

I felt oddly out of place the rest of the day once they led me away from the creature's place of *rest*.

Looking over my shoulder, I wondered more about the realm of the dead.

Thus began such fascinations and discovery.

My mother wasn't too fond of my exposure to hunting, even though my father and brother saw an opportunity in the family business.

Keeping true to my word, I never hunted again. I *honored* the dead. Though it wouldn't be the last experience I had with a dead body. As I grew taller, I learned more, and my once-small view of the world widened. I developed my knowledge about death and learned just how close and personal it could be. After all, my father did run a funeral home.

Poa's Mortuary Services.

My early exposure varied differently from my siblings. My brother didn't mind it, and my sister refused to be near the dead more than necessary. As the middle child, I was the one who was overlooked, yet I took it as an opportunity.

Amongst the funerals and death, I became eerie and wild with my obsessions. It led to my love of academics and exploration of nature.

My father often noticed the graves I made in the woods whenever there was a dead rodent, smiling to himself. He knew it was my doing because of the familiar way things were buried, with some weeds above the ground and a stick.

Mother preferred the hospitality of guests over body preparation; she did the setups for the services and viewings, providing comfort to the families who entered our funeral home. Body preparation unnerved her, reminding her of her own mortality. My sister was like her in that sense; she feared the dead because it made her think of what would come to her one day. My mother hated the idea of having two morbid daughters in the family—*one was bad enough for her*—so it was a relief to her that my sister and I differed. Though it did strain the relationships in our family.

Meanwhile, I was drawn to it—*the dead*. I remembered my father's words about how the dead deserved all the care and respect. *Or else I'd be haunted by the spirits.* My father's fear of being haunted drifted into my own. I couldn't let that happen.

Once I was old enough to assist, he taught me the ways of being a mortician. In secret, of course. No one could know about a girl working with those who have passed on; *it was taboo*. I got my free-spiritedness from him though, so he was more than happy to break all the rules.

"It's like you were born for this, Ella," he would go on to say each time I succeeded in various parts of body preparation.

He withheld parts of the embalming process because of the dangerous chemicals, but I aided in other ways, such as cleaning.

The body preparation process involved delicate care while maintaining modesty of the decedent. In simpler terms—first, there would be a general analysis of the body and what specific fluids would be needed, and then the cleaning process would begin. There was a first bath, which also included the trimming of the nails and hair. The embalming process began after that, depending on what specific fluids were needed. I wasn't involved with that until I was in my adolescent years.

Immediately after, the second bath happened. Cream was applied to the face for moisturization. Then, more or less, the decedent was dressed and transferred to the casket for makeup and layout preparation for viewing services.

Not one body dies exactly the same, I realized. The only constant was the end. That is the cycle in life: morbid to some, but practical to others. *To me.*

Some bodies that came through had met unfortunate ends, while others were more peaceful in their deaths, such as old age or passing in their sleep. I treated everyone who came through the funeral home with the utmost care, whether young or old. I found a sense of duty in caring for the dead, even though my mother and sister found it depressing.

Death didn't have to be a scary, looming thing. I found beauty in it. My father was the same, and my brother just viewed it as a necessary thing for the business.

School was mostly uneventful for me in my youth. It was hard to make friends being the *quiet girl.* Also, no one wanted to talk about funeral homes and death, not when there were gendered toys to play with. The old hearse scared others, too. There were not too many cars in the town of Morella since it was an old mountain town secluded from the rest of the world, unlike the closest big city a couple of hours away. Morella was a world of its own, with gothic architecture and stone buildings with gray stoned sidewalks—frozen in a time before my existence.

People knew who my father was, and kids didn't want to play in a graveyard. I was Morella's social outcast, unlike my sister. As we went through school, although being in separate grades, Mackenzie and I drifted apart, and her social standing was different; she didn't want to be seen with me.

On the other hand, my brother became the jack of all trades, deciding to go off to law school, which left my father and I doing most of the work alone, along with his hired help from another funeral home on the opposite side of town.

My mother began to develop health problems with lots of local doctor visits in the middle of my teenage years. She spent more time in bed than she did with grieving families. I had to float around awkwardly between guests at services and aiding in the basement where the preparation was done, along with my sister's reluctant help.

The years of my youth rolled on, and the stress from dealing with my mother's ailments began to wear on my father, causing his adoring smile to falter into something more somber. His happy appearance gave way to aging gray.

During those years, I realized Mackenzie was more suited for the viewing services. The comforting of others wasn't my forte, not like my sister as she exuded a consoling kindness. I merely *pretended* while dealing with the tears of families and friends that came through for the deceased.

It was easy to read the room and the people in it. It was like people wore masks, sometimes more than one, and other times, it was hard to discern what was real. I got along with the dead more than the living. So, I found it more unnerving to be the social woman and the face of my father's business when people came through the viewing room and the chapel.

The deceased have a story, just like the living. The end of the story is their death, but their life tells another.

I could tell if people were lonely or cruel by how many showed up and their shared stories. I could tell during the body preparation that not everyone truly knew the people they mourned.

As unsettling as it was to think about, I realized no one but my own family would show up to my funeral. Well, *maybe*. It was both disturbing and comforting to ponder. I wouldn't want anyone pretending to like me to show up after I was gone when they didn't show up for me in life. The falsity of that unsettled me. Would more than four people show up to mourn me? Or would it just be my brother and father?

Would they even mourn me?

I was withdrawn and quiet. I only showed my true nature to the dead I served. A mere shell to the land of the living.

Society always decides where people belonged; who was I to change my role?

E.G. POA

CHAPTER TWO

DEATH LIKE ME

ARDELLA — *Past*

School at the Academy of Morella was somewhat uneventful. Until around when I celebrated my seventeenth birthday anyway.

It started with a featherbrained boy and his prying mind.

Many, if not most, ignored me at school, but not *him*.

There I was, enjoying the late summer afternoon on a Friday. It was under my favorite large, lonely eerie tree with its sprangled dark branches keeping shade around it in a perfect circle on the school grounds. My legs were tucked under me as I doodled and wrote in my journal, leaning against the rough bark of the trunk.

We had uniforms at school with pleated skirts, tall socks, and white button-down shirts with a tie and blazer. We had the option of black or dark plaid colors with matching ties and black shoes. That day, I had chosen black with a plaid white skirt and a white button-down. The tie was lazily loosened while I used my black blazer for something to sit on. My pale blonde hair was down instead of up in a bun like it usually was.

I was lost in thought, etching random skulls and words relating to death, when a tall figure appeared in my periphery.

"What are you scribbling there?" A deep, curious voice made my pen pause.

It took me a moment to respond as I slowly took in his dark looks, dressed in all black with glimmering blue eyes and matching dark hair. His black tie was also hanging loosely. My mind wandered more. How had I not noticed him before? *Did I ever notice anyone outside of death and art?*

I began to appreciate all I saw of him until I landed on those eyes that tore through me. I ignored the way my heart raced. *He had to be dark like me, then.*

I wiggled my pen between my fingertips. "Do you want the truth or a well-crafted lie?"

His amused chuckle echoed low, and the sound of it brought heat to my cheeks.

What sane person would want to talk so casually to someone like *me?* The black sheep, or *the odd one with yellow eyes.*

Perhaps it was his dark looks, or our possible shared morbidities.

"The truth."

I closed the notebook, my pen holding my place, and sighed deeply.

"I'll spare us both the trouble. You have eyes; you can see how I partake in most activities solo. I adore the peculiarities, things no one else does. All the dark and taboo things..."

He flopped down next to me, *clearly uninvited,* a clever smile placating his lips. "Go on. Like what? What kinds of things?"

I stared at those eyes, unable to look away. He was so close to me, closer than anyone ever dared. *Why* was he so close to me?

Debating with myself, I sought those blue sapphire-like pools staring back at me, not easily swayed.

"Death."

His lips curled with intrigue; a cute boyish look came through.

"So, you're fascinated with death like me. That's cool. It makes you more appealing in my book." His gaze never left mine, secrets brimming as if I were the key to his locked door.

I wondered where such a door would lead.

God, he was so handsome.

I had the natural social skills of a *dead* rabbit. Practically nonexistent.

Being forced to smile and listen to grieving families wasn't the same thing—*not by a long shot.*

"Welcome to the odd club where I'm the only member." My lips threatened to smile big, but they curled ever so slightly to one side.

He stuck out his hand. "The name is Rigswold. Call me Rigs."

I awkwardly shook it. "Ardella."

My heart began to race at the warmth his hand exuded. *Why. Was. He. So. Close?*

"I've never heard such a name before. It's beautiful, just like the girl that bears it."

Damn. He's good.

I turned away, blushing, not knowing what to say.

"Since you were truthful, it's my turn," he went on to say, interrupting my moment of shyness.

I turned to look at him, a single brow raised on where he was going with his statement.

He scooted closer, nearly flush to my side. My knees were

touching his legs. His smokey earth scent enveloped me immediately. *It was not unwelcome.*

"Have you ever been kissed before, Ardella?" His eyes moved from my blank stare as I processed his words, and then his eyes locked onto my lips. "I would very much like to do that with you."

Does he just walk up to people and say that? My God!

Stumped, I was completely out of it. My brain ceased all function.

I stammered. "I—uhh..."

A low sound escaped him. "I take that as a *no?*"

I began to sweat. *Who does this guy think he is?*

"N-no. I h-have not," I somehow managed to get out, answering his first question and ignoring the second.

"Are you against it?" He smiled, and *goddamn that blushing of mine.*

"Are you being serious?"

He nodded, blatantly moving in for it. "Your cute blushing isn't changing my mind either."

God bless it.

My heart was *really* running for it, and he was bold. It made me wonder what that was like. *I could never be as bold as he was.*

When his lips suddenly touched mine, I relished the softness.

I clutched my leather-bound journal for dear life. As if it could offer me comfort in such a moment. Fireworks exploded in my mind, awakening me to something new and unfamiliar. A star was forming in my bloodstream, and a strange sensation traveled down to the pit of my belly. There was so much newness for one afternoon, and it was more overwhelming than listening to people talk and ramble at the mortuary viewings.

When Rigs pulled away, I began to wonder if I was

dreaming. That's what it was, wasn't it? *I must be sleeping under the tree.* Why on earth would some random boy want to *kiss* me?

"How was that?" He asked softly, eyes half-lidded and seemingly content with himself.

Okay, he's too good at this. Too smooth.

Bashfulness seeped back in, and I was bewildered by the whole experience.

"I have nothing to compare it to. I'm sorry," I told him honestly, growing quieter.

His face softened, leaning back in to murmur against my swollen, freshly kissed lips. "Practice makes perfect then. I'm not here for only *one* kiss."

I scoffed, and he pulled me back in, hand cupping my cheek. Lips still soft, they became hungrier, more eager. His tongue slipped in to tangle with my own, a strange dance that I somehow understood the rhythm to.

Naturally, that tree would become my favorite for more reasons than just the quiet.

Not knowing how long our lips were joined, we pulled away breathlessly sometime later. My insides were going wild, overstimulated by my first kissing experience.

Rigs bit his lip; his blue eyes were brighter somehow. "Come, read me what you wrote."

He pulled me closer, and I was quickly wrapped in his warmth as his arm circled me. His smoky scent was stronger the closer he got. I found comfort in it and leaned into him as I read the page I was working on.

"The dream of death is not raging and violent, for she speaks in whispers in the night. Luring me into the void she brings."

"So, Death is a woman?" He asked quietly as I turned my face when his fingers lightly brushed against my arm.

Goosebumps lingered in the wake of his light caress.

"Is she not?" I countered back, curious about how he viewed death.

Instead, my heart stopped when he smiled. "Indeed, she is... You're as captivating in your looks as you are with your haunting words."

I smiled back genuinely for the first time in a while; his lips met mine eagerly once more. Only that time, I was ready for them.

Even at our first meeting, I knew something had bloomed within me, whether it was dark flowers of possible growth or a first possible relationship with someone.

It was a better afternoon when he joined me and captivated me with a single look and softness I wasn't used to.

Maybe my later teen years wouldn't be so bad, after all.

I lied before.

Death was not a woman. It was a man coming to take me away into the night.

At least, that's what Rigs did to my heart.

O' MAMA

Death will last
    Always the walking ghost,
    even in the afterlife
    Did you love me in the past?
    Death will last
    Yearning for something long past
    There's only this knife
    Death will last
    Always the walking ghost, even in the afterlife

— E.G. Poa

E.G. POA

CHAPTER THREE

DEATH SPARES NO ONE

ARDELLA — *Past*

When my mother died, it rained. The cool drops wrapped me in a static embrace, drowning out everything else. It was shortly after I began dating Rigswold.

My family remained silent during her service, except for my sister's wailing. Somehow, I couldn't find it within me to shed tears. All I could focus on was the steady drizzle of the day.

My father did her makeup and put her in her favorite dark blue dress as he allowed no one else to touch her. Everyone found him to be slightly mad, and perhaps he was. He was shut in all night with her, and I could hear his muffled sobbing and muttering from upstairs. As weird as the house and life were, my father still loved my mother.

Rigswold's warm hand was the only grounding support I needed during the service. An odd silence droned on once the services finished as I stood there staring at her grave with people around me in black. *Where was that support while she was sick?*

I didn't remember the preacher's words or quoted scripture. I wasn't listening to him, or God; just the buzzing in my ears surrounding her death.

My mother, an empty shell of a vessel. Dead. *Gone.*

She had been a living ghost for years since she got sick. She was already so pale, wasting away in the dark depths of her room.

Mother. It was just a title. I came from her womb, *screaming into this life.* One I didn't ask to be born into. How could I figure out what I was meant for when the answers were left in her grave? She poured her love into my sister, saving none for me.

So goes life, I guess.

No wonder I couldn't feel anything about her passing. There was judging looks from outsiders for my lack of tears while my sister showed out for the both of us.

My brother disappeared after the burial, and my father drank himself into a slumber.

It was the first night Rigs stayed over.

We didn't do anything untoward but hold each other while rain slapped against my window. Its sounds and his steadying breaths were all I could focus on. I found a sense of peace there in his arms while thankful for the company during her funeral. My mind was empty, focusing on nothing but the body next to mine that was still breathing.

"You're not alone; I'm here for whatever you need of me," Rigs whispered into the dark of my room.

Rubbing his arm, I turned and curled up against his chest, wrapping an arm around him as he did the same.

"Thank you. I'm merely processing, but I couldn't have done it without you today."

His hand ran through my hair tenderly.

"I wouldn't be anywhere else today than by your side. The next few months will be difficult, but we'll get through it together."

I let his words wash over me and sink in. While grateful, I still found myself sinking further into the pit, only held together by his touch.

The rain suited my mood for its cold melancholy and reminder that *sometimes mother nature cries for you because you can't feel anything at all.* Some deaths were shocking or expected, and others...*just happened.* There were no answers to why things happened other than to just sit with it. So, I mind-numbingly sat with it. Bitter and cold.

According to Mackenzie, my moods were typical for girls my age. *A teenager near adulthood.* It only made me internalize my mother's death more. She still wept, realizing I would not replace our mother's love. Whatever closeness we once held in youth, it vanished as we withdrew into ourselves and other interests.

I ended up writing a lot; it aided me from exploding—from what I couldn't say. I felt a sense of energy I couldn't shake. *Teenage hormones, I suppose.*

My father ended up giving me the unfortunate birds and bees talk after he sobered up and discovered Rigs in the kitchen the next morning. Birds and bees don't fornicate, so I found the talk repetitive; we also learned about it educationally. *Awkwardly so.*

He did, however, follow the talk with the mention of what rape was and how men like to do it to unsuspecting women who appeared frail and docile. However, as a *secret* mortician, *I* knew all sorts of tricks, like how to bury the dead or to hide them under someone else in their final resting place in the ground...

As the months drew on, my father eventually approved of Rigswold, saying we matched well. Rigs didn't find our home... repulsive or gloomy. So, I naturally agreed with my father's statement. *My boyfriend* was most amused by my father's approval, but was flattered, nonetheless.

In fact, there was nothing I found that I didn't like about him. Rigs listened to my morbid stories and wrote with me. In the spring, we went to the local theater and watched live plays as often as possible.

We spent time under the tree during the summer, unless I had to help out at home. I was hopelessly in love with him, and he stuck around even when I officially emerged into adulthood at age eighteen alongside him.

Before school started for senior year, Rigs and I began our ritual of kissing under that large, familiar tree. I climbed into his lap and slipped my tongue into his mouth while he either held me or let his hands roam. I finally found something better than death. *His touch.*

Although he wasn't much older, he taught me a lot. How to kiss, touch, and *feel.* It was a broad scope that expanded my horizons from my singular vision of death. His long fingers caressed the coldness I once felt, turning it into human emotion. A concept that didn't always register in my mind, which was why I had trouble reconciling it with my odd upbringing. My father's love was the only love that grounded me to *feelings* like the rest of the world. Until my mother got sick anyway.

As an adult, it was time to figure out life and what I wanted to do with it.

The first step was *physical* things with my boyfriend. The need to explore those desires.

It began for the first time after darkness fell with oral sex under *our* tree. It happened after school hours when our peers couldn't see what we did in the shadows. It was simple with how Rigs coached me on his likes.

"Grip it." He moved my hand, showing me how to squeeze his cock in the way he liked. "Yes, just like that."

He showed me the stroking motion, groaning as I did it without his help.

"What next?" I asked, curious about his reactions and feeling my heat from within.

He tried to laugh, but it came out strangled with soft sounds coming from him.

"Well, you can lick it or suck it. No teeth; curl your lips around your teeth."

Thinking of his words, I said, "Don't bite it off—got it."

So, I moved my hand away and experimented with licking his tip, and he stiffened before moaning. Feeling like I was doing something right, I took him into my mouth, tucking my lips over my teeth. I heard his soft sigh as I took note of the salty taste of him and how hard yet soft his cock felt. Without being told, I used my hand as he showed me and continued.

Wet heat flooded between my thighs as he cursed, watching me before his head upturned with another quiet sound.

"I'm going to come soon. I'm told it's a salty taste...just so you're aware."

Appreciating his warning, I closed my eyes and slobbered all over him, and it seemed to drive him wild as I did.

He jolted quickly, and my eyes shot open, thinking something was wrong, and that's when I tasted it. The liquid sputtered out of him in wet, warm shots. I swallowed down the salty taste of him, not at all bothered by it. Instead, I was reminded of the slickness between my thighs. Clearly, I enjoyed it as much as he did.

By the time it was my turn to receive, Rigs had shown me a light where there was none before. What release felt like, and how it was unlike anything I ever experienced. Death swept in, a dark embrace, as he sucked the soul from my center, and I was resurrected as he took me to newer heights.

"Yes, lay down, relax, and leave the rest to me," he instructed as I leaned against the tree trunk, exposing myself bare underneath.

"Fuck, do you normally not wear underwear? That's the sexiest sight, Ardella."

I tugged on my lip as he lay on his stomach and wrapped his hands around my thighs. The sight of it confused me, yet it was not bad either.

My heart was thumping hard in anticipation until the flick of his tongue. I stiffened initially, before he did some magic trick with his lips, sucking on a bundle of nerves—my clit.

A gasp left me as my hands shot out to find something to hold on to. I raised one hand to hold the tree for dear life as my thighs twitched and my eyes rolled back. I did not realize a high like that was possible, yet he did it with his mouth.

Moaning louder than intended, I bit my other free hand to stifle it. I didn't want to get caught out in the open, yet part of me was thrilled by the prospect of being seen.

Then, there was a strange building sensation, like when I rode in the hearse about to go down a steep hill; there was the sensation of falling, until I did, right back toward the ground. I convulsed briefly, crying out and cradling Rig's head to my center.

"I will definitely be doing that again. Fuck me," he groaned, kissing my inner thigh afterward. *I was panting, trying to clear my head.*

"I love you, Ardella."

Strangely enough, I believed him.

He licked his lips, praising me for how I tasted on his tongue before he helped me up, and we gathered our stuff to head to his home.

No one was at his house when he brought me back to it. Eagerly, he took me to his room and lit a single three-wick candle. I found the lighting seductive as we stripped naked. I lay at the edge of his bed, ignoring his room and the dark color of the bedding beneath me, and all I saw were those dark cerulean eyes.

"It hurts the first time, but it will pass. Tell me to stop, and I will, okay?"

My heart pooled into a puddle over his words as I nodded, and he steadied himself between my thighs before slowly easing in. I remembered his statement once he was fully seated, and it felt like I was being torn in two, a strange death to my pussy.

I released a muffled cry as he paused, and I gently encouraged him because if he stayed still, I might've died.

"You feel amazing, Ardella," he said, leaning to kiss me before letting those eyes linger longer.

The sweetness made me focus more on his movements, and the pain eventually subsided and became more pleasurable.

At that, I wrapped my legs tight around him and pulled him down to meet my lips once more, and we shared a moan. I could see the shadows of us dancing seductively around the room as he rolled me over until I was on all fours. I quickly found out how it was a favorite position as he hit deep.

That first night together began the first of many. I rejoiced in how he fell apart with a moan or softly sighed when his cock was in my mouth or the look of love as he gazed into my eyes, seducing me under his dark spell.

He was my first, my raven in the night. My only friend. My dark lover. The savior of my black heart.

We began to speak about the future ahead, after graduation from The Academy. We began to see what it was like to dream, filling whatever void we held from our youth. We talked of marriage, possible children, and many years together. I didn't think it was possible to experience emotions to such a level after my mother's passing, instead of loneliness and longing or my *morbid obsessions*. Rigs encouraged my creativity and becoming one with the heart within my chest.

However, those dreams soon died.

His parents were killed in an accident, and I remembered standing outside his home. I watched as he left with strangers in dark clothing. He had no siblings, no other family besides me. He needed to live with someone until graduation, so placement elsewhere needed to be found since he had nowhere else to go; wherever that was, I'd never know.

That's the day I cried. I never saw him at our tree again.

The people taking him away let him speak to me one last time. Tears streamed down his face as I told him how sorry I was for our unfortunate situation of parting.

"I will cherish what we had, Ardella, but death waits for no one. Maybe I'll see you again someday. When life is different and not so full of death."

He pulled me into a hug, kissing me one more time. I broke down there, watching him walk away to the black car the strangers stood beside. My heart was cracking and ripping at the seams.

Rigs climbed into the vehicle with a look of melancholy, a familiar one I knew all too well as it tore open the void.

A black hole of nothingness.

It was the day I discovered what true loss was.

Death is a promise to everyone and everything that breathes.

I slightly disagreed. Death was not the thing to fear; it was living that was hard. *Surviving, after you are left alone in the world.*

I had no room left within; I was completely emptied.

There was no way I could let myself love anyone else. It hurt too much, and I wasn't sure I could endure such a tragedy again.

I was just like my mother, a ghost held together by my grief, not truly living.

Rigs brought out something new and alive within me. To have it ripped away by sudden misfortunes, I took solace once more in the dead, demanding my father to stop the bullshit of making me do the hospitality I loathed.

Thankfully, it didn't take too much convincing.

"I missed having you around with me, Ella. Reyn can help your sister. I called him back home."

I gave him a forced smile and got to work. Life continued like that for the remainder of the year until I graduated from the Academy of Morella.

Unsure if I would get into any colleges, fate intervened. I found a school in the big city, far away from Morella. I decided to learn more about science and writing. I had a lot to say, and society be damned, I would fucking say it. I needed a change before I wasted away like my mother.

That wouldn't do.

Death waited for no one, and I wasn't sure how to properly live.

But I craved more. I *needed* more.

E.G.POA

CHAPTER FOUR

MORE ODD THAN DEATH ITSELF

ARDELLA — *Past*

Science was positively thrilling. I learned more about anatomy, physiology, death, and the biological scientific approach. My upbringing and exposure made me an excellent candidate for the biology program. Since women were supposed to take more *caretaker* roles, no one second guessed my motives—*little did they know a mortician was already amongst them.*

College was my freedom. I realized I wasn't truly living in Morella. Well, not when I was surrounded by the dead more than the living.

There were no bullies in college, even if I did get odd looks over my strange yellow eyes. However, I made a friend who wasn't swayed away by them. The lovely Anabel Lee. She was in the biology program, too. We were much alike, and such a connection to another female had never existed before then. Our friendship was like the spring, blooming and colorful. It was the floral arrangement over my tomb.

Anabel enjoyed my stories of the mortuary home I grew up

in. She cried with me when I spoke of Rigs, and she aided in healing the brokenness left behind from my youth. The distance away from my father began to wear on me, yet Anabel was the light in the dark room of my mind.

We were the light and the dark; my pale hair versus her black hair. It was most amusing, not only to us but also to everyone else we encountered. She was the second person I shared my creativity with, and she encouraged me to continue. I loved her for that alone, as if she weren't already incredible by simply existing alongside me.

Our dorm was one of the older gothic buildings, hidden amongst trees just outside the campus. That little heathen exposed me to the parties and tomfoolery held in our building alongside others. Absinthe and sex, such dark dreams unfolded.

A large party was being held after midterms, and we dressed promiscuously like everyone else in short black dresses. Walking over to the place where it was held, we linked arms, plotting and planning like two criminals. We were each other's wing woman, and we enjoyed watching and being watched.

"Okay, I want to get laid tonight, and I wouldn't mind seeing that sweet ass of yours either." She wiggled her eyebrows as I huffed a laugh, shaking my head.

"My little slut. Of course, I wouldn't mind seeing you either," I said playfully, catching her shameless grin before I started mimicking her moaning from the last party we went to where we shared a room with two other men.

She laughed while swatting at me. "I do not sound like that!"

With a smug look of my own, I countered, "It's pretty fucking close."

She tried to mimic my moaning, and we began to bicker while laughing hysterically.

We were outside the place where the party was being held, trying to catch our breaths from laughing.

"I love you, Ardella. The only friend I'd ever sleep with and next to while being so comfortable and safe to do so. You are my best friend, bitch."

I took a deep breath, giving her a fond look, and holding out my hand that she took gladly.

"I love you, too. I agree completely. I don't like most women, but you're not most, are you?"

She leaned back and kissed my cheek. "Neither are you. Now, let's go get laid."

I smacked her ass and chuckled, linking our arms again as we prowled inside.

While women were often overlooked, two women together were often fetishized. It was unfortunate, but Ana and I used that to our advantage. College men loved it, and so did we.

No longer was I that quiet, awkward teenager. I wasn't *too* promiscuous, but I was more comfortable in my skin. Anabel was to thank for that. She brought me to life in a different sort of manner than Rigswold did. Anabel Lee aided with not loathing socializing entirely. I still preferred the quiet, but it didn't drive me as mad to be amongst the noise.

The city was a different planet entirely than the mountains I grew up in. Fast paced, and male driven. There were more opportunities and jobs to prosper in, yet it was noisy—*always noisy.*

It made me appreciate Morella more with its lush forest, beauty, and quietness. It was a reminder of all that remained for when I finished school.

Father and I would write letters every so often, and he wanted to know if I would be back home before Mackenzie grew up too much and left home, too. He was lonely. I could tell by the way he wrote his letters, simple and somber. It wasn't the father I knew and loved or remembered either.

According to him, Reynolds was busy supporting the household since my father cut back on the business of death. Kenzie was busy with boys and school, according to him, and wasn't staying home long enough to assist anymore. He couldn't do all the jobs by himself, not that there were many bodies either. Most of the business went to the other funeral home on the opposite side of town.

The family business wasn't looking good, seemingly going under.

In one of my letters, I mentioned how I would be finished with school before Kenzie graduated, and I'd be happy to help him and aid in the basement once more. He seemed pleased at that. His letters to me became more hopeful as I neared my college graduation.

It was during my last year that an ad in the paper caught my eye.

Writer wanted.

The position was flexible, ranging from being a critic to creating stories. The college worked with a private person who held a writer's column that needed to be filled since the current one quit. Such a position allowed me to submit the writings by paper in the mail so I could go back to Morella and still work. There was also a sense of secrecy, allowing me to disguise who I was. It would be cash pay sent via mail. Probably too good to be true, though, but I decided to try anyway.

My blood raced at such prospects as I eagerly raced to my dorm to scribble down various samples, ranging from dark to happier topics like...*flowers and clouds.*

I pulled them from the shallows of my mind, hoping that after staring at the pages for hours, the columnist would appreciate my darker works rather than the sweet ones. I was darkness disguised as light, yet I couldn't disguise it permanently.

Society was still mostly male driven, so I used a pen name. I submitted my work under E.G. Poa. The job would offer creative freedom, and I craved such niceties.

It was a dream, a need for expressionism. *For my written art in the world, it would give me more purpose and meaning.* I needed people to see different perspectives, to ponder outside such mundane lives. I craved the poetry of words like I needed oxygen in my lungs.

To my surprise, I received my letter of acceptance the following week.

Anabel and I got drunk, throwing a huge party, disguising it as an everyday occurrence rather than a job. It was early the following morning when I woke up tangled between two men, smirking as I drank the hair of the dog to wake up and function. I could still feel the lingering kisses and soreness from being filled to the brim by them... Moans and soft sighs from all of us, and orgasms to die for. The party life would end once I graduated, and with another buzz settling in and curing me of my hangover headache, I wandered the old drafty stone building like a ghost before dawn came and went.

My first writing assignment was critiquing another writer, who went by the name of Gildus Furrows. The guy wrote well enough, so my critique wasn't insulting. However, *Sir Gildus* decided to stir the pot he created out of jealousy and folly. Thus, the war began between us, slowly at first, before it grew and grew like wildfire.

The Boss Man warned me about it via letters and notes with my cash pay. However, a little rivalry never hurt anyone, according to him. No man would run me out of where I belonged. *No one.*

So, I didn't hold back. Gildus could jump off a cliff, *the prick.*

It only took a few of my column issues before he started in again. *The absolute audacity of the fucker! Males and their goddamn pride.*

He thought my writings in the column depressing, unrelatable, and inane. To *politely* name a few.

"Poa's latest installment is imposing, offering no insight into the afterlife or death. It is uncreatively drowning with melancholy."

Ana and I would talk shit amongst ourselves in our dorm room. She knew *all* about me, swearing a blood oath to secrecy at 3 am for our secrets to be taken to the grave lest we decided to bless the world with our truths. Ana wasn't a writer, minus the biological research papers we had to do. She was going to try her luck in the city for some hospital opportunities upon graduation, and I told her where to find me if she wanted to visit, *hours away in the mountains.*

My senior year was ending rather quickly. I remained busy between writing creative articles, short stories, and critiquing Prick Furrows. Anabel Lee also kept me busy socially, ensuring I still kept at it. I wouldn't have gotten through anything without her. Another loss I'd have to deal with once we parted ways after graduation. She was my best friend, my soul mate. We were two sides of the same coin, and I couldn't imagine my life without her. Thankfully, she said it wouldn't be the last I would see of her.

Although the year was enticing socially and with my career, peculiar things still occurred, especially with a chance encounter at another university in the nearest city.

Rigswold.

There was an outdoor event with various vendors, and that's where I saw him. *Of all the places to see him.* Rigs was just as handsome, ever more the man than the boy I once knew. The grief hit me at once, reminding me of when he left and how my soul broke apart, particles of dust from a star long past dead.

His arm was around a blonde woman, ushering her and showing her something interesting, I supposed. She wore brighter colors, unlike me in all *gray*. A sparkling ring donned her marriage finger, reflecting the light enough so I caught it when she looked at something in awe. I watched in disbelief, hidden at another stall while they stood at another before kissing under the contrast of the sky.

God spare me.

The woman looked so much like *me*. It was so odd, more odd than death itself. The irony of it... I'm not sure if it was flattery or preservation of what once was but was no more.

I was in public, so there was no way to escape into a small corner to cry. Rigs would be the only man I shed tears for in grief.

Naturally, it wasn't long before I fled toward the train, heading back to the dorm to sulk back into my pit of darkness.

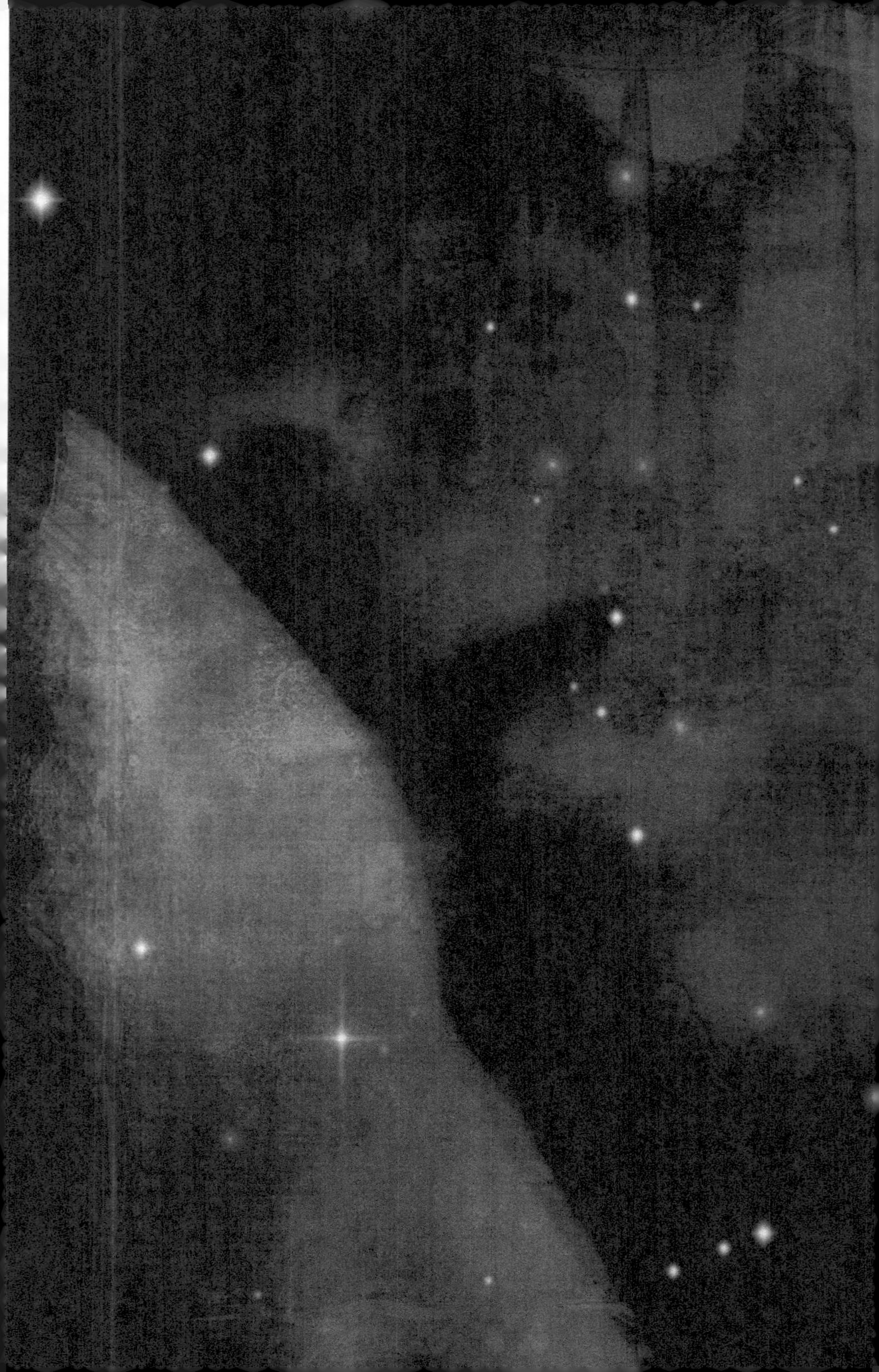

THE MIRACLE

Forged by the atoms of long ago
    There was always more
    To the story
    Of you and me

Paint the sky
    You are my moon and stars
    A carefully crafted place in my heart

Wondrous dreams
    A floating cloud where nothing can reach us
    My secret bargain in the dark

Love is a dream
    Of you and me

The stars are brighter with you around
    There are endless possibilities

The earth beneath my feet is more cherished
    Living is more bearable.

Love is death
    Of all I knew before
    More answers than questions
    The sole focus of you

You have ripped me apart
    Beseeching me
    Heated flesh, rousing touch

The world doesn't seem so small
    In a universe of planets and stars
    We are beautiful and deadly just like them

I began from my mother's womb
    But you are my ending.

— E.G. Poa

CHAPTER FIVE

SO SERENE IN THE MOONLIGHT

ROMAN

It's a prosperous evening of graverobbing.

There's a particular grave rumored to hold expensive gems and trinkets buried with some random elderly woman. So, my brother and I scope it out, hoping to reap the rewards we need.

Thankfully, *the goods* are there. Rubies, sapphires, gold, and silver trinkets fill the casket.

My lips stretch wide at Jackson with utmost glee. "We're going to live well now, Jacky boy!"

The man himself rolls his eyes at me, but I can still see his cute ass grin. He has this shy-boy grin the world falls for, but I know otherwise. He's as depraved as I am. I just don't hide it as well as he does.

I wipe the sweat from my brow, leaning on the shovel as Jack hands me a cloth to carefully move the items into my hip pouch. I give him the shovel as I straddle the open casket unsteadily, trying not to fall the fuck in.

The woman in the casket isn't withering away as I originally thought, having not been in the ground for long with the dirt still fresh. She has her prizes beside her as if she were taking them to the afterlife. *How ridiculous.*

"You won't be needing these where you are, ma'am," I whisper, finishing up with a full pouch weighing down on my hips.

It takes me a good ten minutes before I maneuver myself to close the lid, tapping on it fondly three times in thanks; *my personal ritual that I do each time I take from the dead.*

"I shall honor this gift in creating a better life, ma'am," I say aloud to myself, before Jack reaches down to help me out of the grave.

"Thanks, brother." I give him my thanks as he gets to work with putting the dirt back into the earth.

I stare briefly into the hole where the woman lay in her casket. I would never get used to the fucking putrid smell of corpses. *The worst part of the job.* The stench of rot. I've smelled worse than the old woman in the hole, but it's still enough that I don't like to be in the ground with the dead for long. It gives me the heebie jeebies.

It does make my brother and me money, and it's important to me; to us both. Life's hard enough to get by without it.

"You got the rest of this, right? I'm going to put these in our safe spot so we can get estimates in town tomorrow. That cool?"

"Yeah," he grunts, shoveling dirt as I head out of the cemetery, away from the tombstones and the stench of death.

Jack loves putting things back into place and reburying the bodies. He is odd and eerie in that way, but so am I.

People, in general, are weird. Just as long as it doesn't interfere with me making a living, I don't mind other people's oddities. Truth be told, Jack and I are looking at the mortuary home that is tucked into the woods just outside the central part of Morella. *I bet they have a lot of good shit.*

Many people want their loved ones buried with their favorite things. That means I'm not the only one who likes nice things and money. Like everywhere else, there are rich and poor, and then there are men like me who don't belong anywhere. At least Jackson has brains and reads books. Me?

Well, I'm trouble. I love causing it, and I like being involved in it. A criminal answer, and perhaps I am to some. I wouldn't want it any other way, though.

Sure, money is always at the top of my list, but the second? Sex.

God, do I *love* to fuck. Male or female. Jackson is the same way, except I'm more open about fucking. He's a gentleman, while I'm a pain in the ass; *his ass, I'm sure.*

Thinking about the lame lay I had last night at the only shitty motel outside of downtown, I cut through a path in the woods. *I don't think the woman made any notable noises, so there's that... I know my dick fucking works.*

Sighing to myself, the shadows of the trees are my only comfort, along with the goodies around my hips. It's quiet except for the owls above and the crunch of leaves under my boots. The temperature dropped enough to give me a slight chill. Although, the woods by all the cemeteries around Morella give an eerie air, as if I'm not alone. For a town in its own seclusion in the mountains, it certainly doesn't help its morbid aura. All the odd and unfortunate things that go bump in the night like me. Perhaps the dead are just as disappointed in my life choices and occupations.

The rushing echo of water alerts me as I pause, taking note of the direction it's coming from. Through the thicket of the trees, there are clouds above, with the moon beginning to creep out of them. With that, there's a great internal debate on whether to wash off my face and hands from the dirty deed of the evening.

There's nothing and no one around me, and I could do it unbothered at this time of night. I follow the sounds of trickling water until I make my way down a little hill to the bank. Sighing in relief, I crouch down, scooping the cool water and washing the dirt away before splashing my face. The previous tiredness from digging eases away from me with the cold jolt of refreshing water. I wait for the dirt to move away by the faint current before I take a drink.

Damn, I'm thirsty.

Exhaling in relief, feeling better with the stop, I stand there, taking in the surroundings as more moonlight seeps from behind the clouds. The creek isn't as small as I thought and looks like a good bathing spot. The quietness is peaceful, something I can appreciate out here.

I stare further down the bank off into the distance. The moon comes out fully then, and something catches my eye in my side vision.

Running a hand through my hair, I squint more, looking off to my right.

Trying to get a better look, my eyes adjust. The light rushing of the water seems to ease off into another spot, opening up to a calmer body of water. Could it be a lake or something, maybe? A blur of white catches my attention, and curiosity gets the best of me. *As it always does.*

Making sure my pouch is still tight at my hips, I carefully climb the little hill and follow the water's direction. The rushing sounds grow quieter, and that's when I realize someone *is* bathing in the larger area.

It takes a few more moments for my eyes to adjust fully to the blinding moonlight and stark contrast shadows of the trees.

The closer I get, the more I pause, hidden away up on the hill. I can't be seen or be heard.

I notice neatly folded clothes on the bank. Not able to tell quite yet, I observe the larger area of water, eager to figure out just *who*'s in the water. Especially at this time of night, in the dark... A morbid creature unafraid of the dark, like myself.

A short silence passes before a figure rises from the water. There's a halo effect of the water, and the moon illuminates the head of long, white hair.

Fuck.

Frozen in place, all I can do is watch.

The person has their back to me, and I can't see too much past the pale hair until they swim and stand. There's a pale glow on their skin, and breasts bask in the light. A light splash catches my attention while I take in those lovely tits. Especially when she leans back into the water, letting herself float.

My dick has a mind of his own as I watch, greedy for more. I *love* to watch, silent and passive, as if I don't exist to the unsuspecting person being observed.

I admire how long her legs are, glistening in the water. Pale, dainty arms stretch out beside her. An angel in water, free and floating.

Who is this woman? Why is she bathing at night alone? Does she have a death wish? Or does she simply not give a fuck?

My kind of woman, either way.

I wrestle with myself, staring at her tits that are begging for my tongue. She's alone, ready for the taking... Yet, I'm not *that* depraved. Or cruel. I don't rape women, even if I am imposing on someone's privacy. A fine line, I guess. How the fuck can I get off if the other person isn't having a good time?

I don't understand, so I do something better. I keep watching from the shadows like the pervert I am.

My cock bulges over the answer when I take it out, imagining all the dirty, vile ways I'd defile the angel in water. If the opportunity ever comes to me, of course. Despite my urge to go in there and seduce her with my charms, I settle for jacking off instead. I will not disrupt her peace *tonight*.

Finding some reprieve, I stroke my cock as silently as possible. The peaks of her nipples are rising above the surface along with her milky white thighs. It's all I can think about as I bite my lip, imagining being between them, licking and feeling her around me. Her face is so serene in the moonlight. I can only imagine her face when she screams in pleasure or with her arms wrapped around me, thighs squeezing tight against my skull.

If only.

When she stands once more, still facing me, she begins to wash herself, hands roving over her tits, then down further and further.

The view is all I need to come.

I hold my breath, stiffening while I shoot my load off. A quiet sound of pleasure leaves me; thankfully, it doesn't alert her to my presence. Sighing to myself, I debate whether I want to follow the woman home to make sure no one else has my experience or to leave and continue my business.

It doesn't take me long to decide as I put my cock away, leaning against the thick tree trunk to gather myself.

The detour doesn't matter as I continue to stare at the beautiful woman bathing in the moonlight. She seems so innocent and pure, uncorrupted by the world. As if the peace of the forest gives her all she needs with its nightly serenity. The view is a dream in my dark world.

I stay hidden when she finally steps out of her wet sanctuary. Her clothes are dark, and she carries a sack with the dirty ones. When she leaves, only then do I trail behind her at a distance, careful of my steps and making noises.

I make an oath to myself as I follow her.

If ever given the chance, should I catch her in that water again, I'd go to her. Not like a horny fool, but as someone who happened upon her. I doubt I'd ever get to be too friendly with her, so I couldn't let her know how fucked up I really am.

We walk for about an hour in the opposite direction I'm supposed to be going. My thoughts linger during that timeframe. What would my mother say if she saw me now?

Well, she can't say much since she's dead, killed by my father. Who then pulled the trigger on himself.

A murder-suicide.

How romantic of them.

Ever since I can remember, I don't have much of a memory of my parents. I don't particularly care for parental figures either since being rushed away into a boy's home near the heart of Morella. That's where I met Jack, and we have been inseparable ever since. It was always us against the world, and it always would be. Jackson is my only family blood or not. *We make our own families.*

Distracting my thoughts on my upbringing with Jackson, a familiar modern—but classical—house comes into view, luring me away from my past.

For a funeral home, the place is *huge. Creepy, too.* It holds a dark exterior with a wraparound porch. There are three floors with angled windows and a scary-looking crematorium off in the backyard. It's mostly hidden from the main view unless you are walking around the house, of course. The house itself gives off an eerie vibe that brings about the chills again. Maybe it's haunted?

The crematorium behind it, meters away, certainly doesn't help the appeal.

Who knew it would be the *same* house Jackson and I plan to rob?

I stand back in the tree line as she makes her way into the large, dark house. It looks fucking creepy at night, more so than the daytime. The discovery of this place was merely an accident anyway when the two of us began our search for other cemeteries and graveyards in and outside of Morella.

An unsettling feeling of gloominess washes over me.

Okay, that's my cue. I've wandered long enough.

I wait until the woman is inside before I jog through the woods, hoping I can beat Jack back to our place in the heart of town.

Does the woman live there with her parents? Or siblings? On her own?

I don't know much about it other than it's a place of grief.

People also live there. *Live.* Where the dead are prepared. The Death Service Place.

How anyone can live in the same place they work with the dead is beyond me. Point aside, it has wealth, and that's what Jack and I need to get our own place.

We did odd jobs to get the money and save up.

So close to our goal, so fucking *close.*

More information needs to be discovered about that home of the dead and the family inside.

Jack loves doing research and shit, so I'm betting he will happily help me with it. I won't tell him my fascination, not yet. *It's for research purposes.*

So, if we run into any hiccups when we finally rob the place, we will be prepared to deal with it, assuming multiple people live there.

We don't hurt people when we do bigger robberies on occasion, but sometimes it can result in violence. Gotta save our own asses, after all. We don't rob houses often though, as it's too much of a hassle. We work in the witching hour specifically for those reasons. While the world sleeps, *we do not.*

Thankfully, I make it in before the sun comes up *and* before Jack. My eyelids are drooping, and I put the gems and trinkets away in our safe spot under the floorboard—a large safe box.

Before I can debate on bathing myself, I plop onto my bed, face first, eagle spread—passing out immediately.

My hope is that an angel will appear in my dreams, and the rest will remain to be seen.

E.G.POA

CHAPTER SIX

HANDSOME STRANGERS

After being away from home all these years because of college, it's nice to be back home amongst the dead. I suppose the living too, since my father's still half alive and working at the funeral home.

The quietness is most welcoming, too.

Since it's been years since being home, it begins to feel like I'm visiting an old companion. I miss Anabel already, the puzzle piece that held me together during our college years. What will I do without my partner in crime?

My father greets me at the door on my first weekend back with an aged half-smile.

I bring my bags in from the car that dropped me off, hauling them up to my old room. It's only us in our large house all weekend; my siblings haven't thought to drop by with a hello. Why should they care, anyway, when we haven't spoken in years?

Shrugging over it, my dad finally gets me as aid for preparation in the basement again. To make life easier for him, he had a ramp installed at the backside of the house to make transport quicker and safer for the unloading and loading of the caskets. It wouldn't be seen to the public during viewings, *thankfully*, because funerals were morbid enough for the grieving families.

Morticians have to figure out how to turn off and mask emotions for dealing with grief and body preparation.

Bodies could be heavy depending on who they are with their size, weight, and height; my father is getting older and doesn't have the strength to use the cellar doors and steps anymore. The ramp entry is a godsend for him. Apparently, he had it done after I went off to college, so I don't have much experience with it yet.

My father and I share stories as we work in the basement on a young woman who died of a heart attack in her sleep. *What a way to go.*

She's pale postmortem and in great shape. It puzzles me why someone so healthy died so young.

According to my father, it was hereditary, and the signs weren't caught in time since she was so *seemingly* healthy.

"Sometimes, God calls us home, Ella," he tells me as I carefully do her makeup for the viewing.

She's already in the casket upstairs in the viewing room. The chapel next to it was also extended while I was gone.

"I don't believe in God, Dad," I say matter-of-factly while finishing up the pink lipstick.

He frowns, sighing in defeat.

Why did he sigh like that?

"What do you believe in, then?" He asks quietly, and I scrunch up my brows, observing my finished work.

"Death."

I turn my gaze to him and catch the ghost of a smile.

"There is more to life than death, Ella. You always were my

strange child... It was relieving for a while that you finally got away from all of this."

"Dad." I give him a childish, mild eye roll while crossing my arms.

He shakes his head, not having any of it.

"I'm serious. You are so young. You need to fall in love again and experience life outside this house. Outside all this death. I want more for you. You know, I inherited this place once my brother passed, and Reyn was still a young boy. It was an adjustment for me, and like you, I found all of this curious and fascinating."

After cleaning the brushes and replacing the sponges, I put away the makeup supplies. He keeps me company as I do.

"After twenty years," he goes on, "you start to feel like another body in the morgue. No wonder your mother got sick... There is more to life than this deathly obsession you have, Ella."

It's my turn to sigh.

"Don't even think about blaming yourself. You could've sold this place and gone elsewhere, *both of you*. It's unfortunate that she left this life, but as you said before, *'sometimes God calls us home.'* Don't be so hard on yourself. I do *not* have an obsession. It's called being passionate about something, Dad. I take my joy when I can. I am not who I was when I left here..."

He strides closer, bending down to kiss my cheek.

"You've grown up so much since I last saw you. The city life did you some good."

"You know I like the quiet better."

He pats my head with an amusing laugh. "I know you do. Good job on Miss Morris," he indicates his thumb toward the casket while rubbing my shoulder lightly.

"The people from the church will be here soon," he adds while we finish up the layout of the room together.

The family arrives an hour after we finish, bringing personal effects and double-checking our work on Miss Morris. The family gets their private viewing, approving of my handiwork.

The viewing for everyone else occurs an hour later. It quickly becomes busy, movements rushing by me in a blurry haze. So many people show up for Miss Morris. *I mask my need to disappear from the crowd for as long as I can.*

It only lasts for so long before I venture outside, past the cars lingering near the edge of the property, away from the chatter. My father had some help from the churchgoers, so I don't feel bad leaving him to fend for himself.

I find a tree trunk to put my hand on at the line where the yard and forest meet. The house stands as a looming structure in the distance, with the shadows of the crematorium off behind it.

As long as people don't wander around the property or poke around, they won't be frightened and unnerved by the graveyard and crematory...

There's a slight chill in the air while I realize the lengths my father went through to have my mother buried in our family graveyard. I ignore it most of the time and stay away from the crematory that unnerves me, along with her resting place.

My father or brother usually handled the crematory. There is something about it that makes me stay away, and I wonder if I will ever get over that discomfort. *Probably not.*

I take in the fall foliage around me, grounding myself back into my surroundings and out of my head, a trick Anabel taught me while in one of our psychology classes. It's valuable for someone like me who likes to go away in their mind.

Wrapping my arms around myself, and leaning against the rough tree bark, I listen to swaying branches in the wind while enjoying the quiet outdoors.

A crunching of feet behind me draws me away from my daze.

Turning my head to the side, I take note of how daylight is beginning to fade as a male strides toward me.

"Nice evening, is it not?" I hear the slight baritone voice echo quietly, causing goosebumps to rise on my arms.

"Yes," I answer him simply, turning my head away from the stranger.

"Sorry to disturb you, it was busy in there. It's quieter out here."

Not quiet enough, evidently...

Turning around to face the person, I open my mouth to speak, but words fail me.

The man before me is *gorgeous*.

His reddish hair is curly and messy in a kept way, with glasses framing his handsome face. He appears educated and intelligent even, not that his glasses and attire don't give him away, but one shouldn't make assumptions. The dying light around us makes him appear more charming, along with his stretching smile.

Shit, he caught me staring.

"I am not disturbed or intruded." My eyes rove over him curiously. "Did you know the girl?"

"No, I'm afraid not. I'm merely being a respectful townsperson."

I nod. *At least he's honest.* "How polite of you."

His white shirt outlines strong muscles underneath. I wonder what he does for a living to give him such strength. A part of me begins to envision how he would feel against my fingertips and how his lips taste.

Geez, why am I even thinking about this stranger?

He smiles again, causing me to shiver. A moment later, he

sticks out his hand toward me. "The name's Jackson, but please, call me Jack."

I stare at his hand for a long, awkward moment before reaching out to shake it.

"Ardella."

My hand tingles at his warm touch before he pulls away.

"An unusual name," he tilts his head to take me in, "but beautiful, nonetheless."

Feeling shy and exposed in front of him, I blush, muttering a quiet thanks.

"I only speak the truth."

I suppose you aren't too bad to look at either, Jackson.

Looking at him arouses my body, so I politely excuse myself. "It's lovely to meet you, Jack. I should probably get back in there to make sure I'm not needed."

He offers a lingering smile and inclines his head; I move past him.

His words remind me similarly of what Rigswold had said to me all those years ago, an uncomfortable ache arising in my heart. Jackson isn't Rigs, but I'll probably never see him again; it's best not to get any hopes up or form any attachments.

Without turning back to confirm, I can practically feel his eyes on me, following me as I make my way up the porch steps. I turn to look back once I'm at the door; he's still where I left him.

I blink in surprise, almost as if I had expected to see him disappear, like he hadn't been there at all. He's staring at me, and my insides heat. With a small smile, I give him a little wave before I go inside, back to the chaos.

As it goes, the evening drags on as more and more people finally filter out, quieting down the house. Just when I think I'm in the clear, I walk into my bedroom to grab a book and find some *random male* in there.

"What are you doing in here?" I demand, wondering if I need a weapon to defend against such an intruder.

Turning on the light, the man freezes, remaining at the foot of my bed. Heat rises to my cheeks as he turns around; by God, he's handsome, too.

What is it with my luck tonight?

"Sorry, I was looking for the bathroom."

"Well, it is *clearly* not in here," I say, relief settling within me that I'm able to keep my voice firm.

Opening the door for him to leave, he comments on the way out, "Nice room, by the way."

I catch his smirk and melt, *only a little.*

With a sigh, I narrow my eyes, signaling I mean business to the guy.

Why was he in the dark?

He stands outside the door, looking lost as I point two doors down.

"Right, thank you."

I stand there watching, ensuring he goes until he closes the door behind him.

He must have been looking for something, but *what?*

Quickly taking inventory of my room, nothing appears out of place. Interestingly enough.

My heartbeat is in my ears while I remain at my door until he leaves the bathroom.

The male walks by with a smile as if I didn't just catch him snooping around in my room *in the fucking dark.*

What other oddities will arise?

"Have a good night, *Sunshine,*" he says as he strolls down the stairs unhurriedly.

I roll my eyes, grabbing for my journal, but instead of leaving the house, I check the other rooms on the top floor before sitting at the top of the steps to make sure no other unwelcome guests are sneaking around.

At least the other rooms were undisturbed. Nothing out of place, not even the dust. My siblings certainly missed out on all the excitement. Father didn't hear a word all weekend from either of them.

While I was off at college, Reynolds got his own place and moved out. He became a lawyer while I was away, so he wasn't around, and my sister did her own thing, so she hasn't been back to our home. Since coming back home a week ago, I haven't seen her.

At the end of the night and after the funeral the next morning, I fall into my bed, wondering about those two guys who dared to smile at me. Were they local? Would I see them again?

A venture into town will be a fine starting place. My curiosity is getting the best of me, plus I still have the column writing job, so I need to go into town to mail it off in confidential envelopes anyway.

It's the perfect excuse to run into those handsome strangers.

Either of them would do.

CHAPTER SEVEN

THE DEATH SERVICE PLACE

ROMAN — *Past*

"Hey, perfect opportunity," Jack said, handing me the newspaper.

Poa Mortuary Services, viewing tonight at 5 pm. Alice Morris, 29 Years Old...

"Bingo," I told him wickedly, patting him on the back.

"I'll pretend to have some familiarity with the dead girl if anyone asks, and one of us can cause a distraction if needed while we scope the place out."

I considered him. "Works for me, Jacky. Let's blend in tonight and check it out. I saw a pale-haired woman go in there when I was watching the place the other night."

Jack raised a single brow. "Oh? Do tell."

Ignoring his knowing look, I shrugged, debating with myself how much I wanted to reveal.

"Seems young to me, but it was dark, so anything is possible... That place gives me the creeps," I admitted.

"I'll keep a lookout. We'll need to figure out how many people live there, then re-evaluate our methods from there."

I agreed with him as he walked away with the newspaper, placing it on the table.

"How anyone lives in the same place as the dead is beyond me." A shiver went down my spine at the reminder of the house's eeriness at night, like a silent death awaiting me.

He gave me a slight shrug. "We'll have our own place soon, so who cares? Although, part of me is curious about what that's like too. I wonder if it's strange or fascinating to live in the house of the dead?"

Staring at him in disbelief, I shake my head. *Of course, you'd find it fascinating, you odd man.*

"Ask someone... I don't know."

I checked the time with the old clock on the wall; five wasn't too far off.

"It's showtime," I announced while stripping out of my clothes to change.

We still lived in the large attic space in the group home we grew up in. It had been abandoned by the owners years ago, and we took over the upstairs space. It was the only home we had ever known. Somehow there was still running water and electricity. It probably wasn't the safest place to live, but Jack and I had nowhere else—*no one else.*

I dug through my clothes in the corner and put on something appropriate, as did Jack. A simple gray button-up with a coat that matched the pants.

Once we finished getting ready, we quickly made our way to *Poa's Mortuary Services*, preparing ourselves to blend in with the grieving crowd.

"So, what's your interest in the pale-haired woman?" Jack questioned as we strode through the woods. "Is there one?"

Slouching with defeat, I came clean. "I may have caught

her bathing in the moonlight the other night and followed her home to The Death Service Place."

"Funeral services, Ro," he shook his head, a smile crept up at the corner of his lips over my antics. "A death place... You make it sound like it's a place to die."

"Well...they're already dead," I indicated my hand out beside me, and he rolled his eyes, not leaving me room to bypass the first part of my statement.

"Bathing in the moonlight, hmm? Well, don't leave me hanging."

A low laugh tumbled out of my chest as he waited expectantly while we briskly kept up our pacing.

"It was quite the view, Jacky. Glorious tits and a body deserving of worship. I call first dibs, if anything were to happen in the future."

We paused and gave each other a knowing look as a sly smile slid onto Jack's face.

"Not if I win her over first. She might like me better," he added, as if it were a contest.

"And I'm supposed to be the wild one," I chided him, and his laughter became joyous.

"Must be something in the air tonight."

I circled my arm around, bringing him closer as I squeezed his shoulder with a carefree laugh alongside him.

"*Game on, brother*. If she sees us tonight, or we make some sort of contact, we'll go from there and see who she leans toward."

"And if it's both?" He raised a single brow with that cute ass boyish look I'd come to love and appreciate.

To drive my point home, I smacked his ass with a grin. "Then *you* can *watch*," I teased as he poked my side.

"*Game on, brother*."

Present

Upon arriving at *The Death Service Place*, it's in full swing with people.

I give a saluting nod to Jack, and we separate.

Stepping in the threshold, the viewing room is crowded as I walk in to *pay my respects* to the stranger. People are crying all around me as I pretend to be sad too, and I slowly make my way through the line to view the girl's body. She's only a year younger than me. So seemingly full of life and healthy before she died in her sleep.

The house still gives me the willies, and I do not want to linger here longer than necessary.

It's finally my turn to view Miss Morris. Her hair is strawberry blonde, and she appears to be *sleeping* peacefully. As if her passing is the most peaceful thing she could ever do amongst her pale pink satin pillows in her white dress. Gentle and delicate, never getting to fully live. *Such a shame.*

I quickly move away from the body, feeling weird as I ease my way out of the crowded room. *Geez, this girl knew a lot of people.*

In the foyer, three men are aiding the guests, along with a familiar pale-haired woman. *Goddamn, is she a sight up close in the light.*

Not sticking around for them to notice me, I creep upstairs quietly and scope it out. I find the bathroom, a messy girl's room, and a male's clean but dusty room. There is a locked room and another male's room that appears to be more lived in. The last room is clean, with a bookshelf filled with neutral tones and gray along with the rest of her room. Somehow, I piece together that it belongs to the woman from downstairs.

The messy room didn't seem like her, not when the clothes were folded neatly when I watched her bathe in the moonlight...

It smells so lovely in here.

I lean down to inhale her pillow and covers. There's a light scent, like the fall season amongst us, but sweet too. It is comforting, at the very least.

I turn out the light to keep smelling her covers. I note how I'm already becoming addicted. Lured into her world, unknowingly to the woman herself, yet thrilling, nonetheless. *I wonder what her name is?*

Minutes pass. I move a few feet away to the edge of the bed when she catches me in her room. Watching her accusing glare and how she reprimands me... it *makes me hot.* I want to kiss her immediately when her sultry voice blesses my ears. Her yellow eyes are locked on me.

When she points to the bathroom, I reluctantly leave and remember the part I have to play. I want to know more about the woman with alarming yet piercing yellow eyes. I don't realize their color until seeing her up close as I pass her. *Beautiful.*

Going into the bathroom, I use it and wash my hands. The house has electricity and good plumbing, and money is required for that. They have to have cash or something valuable being stashed somewhere.

At home, on a good day, we get heat or hot water, not the luxury this house holds though. For a spooky house, it has charm inside.

I sigh and look into the mirror, running a hand through my dark hair.

She'll be watching me now; my spying is over for the night.

Finishing up my business, I leave the bathroom, bidding her goodnight and disappearing afterward.

I can't find Jack until an hour later.

Filling him in as we walk back home, he begins to tell me about his evening.

"She's a beautiful creature, I'll give you that. You were right."

Delight fills me with his response. "Oh yeah? Why a *creature* and not a woman?"

He shrugs nonchalantly, ignoring my jab. "With eyes as rare as those, there's no way. She looks otherworldly—*resplendent*. An angel from purgatory."

I raise a brow at him. "While you're not wrong, *dramatic* much?"

"I'm just speaking the truth. Do you think we'll run into her again?"

I sigh. "Fuck, I hope so."

"Me too," he whispers.

We continue the rest of the way home in silence.

Jack put hope in my head. I *need* to see her again. To cure my newfound obsession. Haunting eyes with nearly white hair, the beauty of what I imagine death to be like if I could choose. *If being around death wasn't so off-putting to me—money aside.* Even with our profession of grave-robbing and planning to rob a mortuary—it doesn't help my case.

Until our next course of action, I'll watch her house like usual.

E. G. POA

CHAPTER EIGHT

A BOOKWORM LIKE ME

ARDELLA

The next time there's a sunny day, I go into town.

There were already so many days of dreary, dark clouds and rain that I spent much of the time writing and helping my father.

He even told me I was to take a break when the weather cleared.

I begin my day at the public library, knowing I'll probably remain there until it closes. I debate on where two handsome men would possibly hang out. The one who joined me outside seems to be the type to linger in libraries. Hopefully, it's not too presumptuous of me to assume.

Debating internally over it, I wander around the large, old, brick building. It has gorgeous tall cathedral-like ceilings with two floors and large windows which create lighting that's perfect for a bookworm like me. There are carefully placed chairs that are away from any chatter, along with a few chaises.

The centralized space is still mostly open. The top floor consisted of five sections with romance, fantasy, fiction, young adults, and children. The children's section is closed since it's during the school week. On the main floor has educational books, mystical/occult, classics, and poetry.

The top floor doesn't have the ladders, but the bottom floor does. I rather enjoy the experience of using them, gliding to the next shelf to find beloved books. It's fancy, reminding me of the college library that had them, too. It was much bigger than the one in Morella.

Ana and I would giggle over it, taking turns pretending we were damsels in distress on those moving bookshelf ladders. It brings me joy to use the ladders for no particular reason other than euphoria alone.

Remembering my best friend, I make a mental note to write to her soon, even if it's just to check-in.

I move the ladder through the educational section, trying to find interesting reads.

Adjusting my plaid skirt, I climb up to grab one about the anatomy of the dying process I haven't read, plus another on death and the afterlife. More curious about the latter, I carefully make my way down the ladder, carrying a stack of five titles.

Glancing around the quiet bottom floor, I find the perfect spot tucked near the backside, next to one of the large windows. Settling into an oversized, red velvet armchair, I spend the better part of the day reading a book about the afterlife, filling my mind with information.

The key to the book is how there is no *real* correct answer. Depending on religious or spiritual beliefs, those answers vary. Philosophers and dreamers hypothesize such novelties, but the reality of what comes after death is unknown. Once you are dead, *you're dead.* It's fascinating to read the viewpoints either way.

Marking my page, I recall a section on various types of witchcraft and necromancy. The hunt begins as I climb the ladder in another section to find more books about witchcraft, necromancy, and astrology.

To my surprise, I find a couple of books on each. I smile to myself over the finds before realizing I have overextended the stack in my hands when it drops down to the floor.

Well, shit!

Cursing to myself, I grumble and climb down, only to find the person I've been wishing for all day.

What's his name again?

James? Jake? Something with a J... Ja—*Jack!* That's right!

He's kneeling, examining a couple of the books, and part of me wonders what his thoughts on the topics are, or if I'm simply a freak in his eyes.

At the bottom of the ladder, he carefully holds them in his arms. A slow gaze travels up from my black shoes to my tall socks, the skin on my thigh, and the plaid skirt. I heat over that gaze while he rises to meet mine.

He reminds me of a schoolboy with his suspenders and glasses, looking handsome with his red curls. Since I have a better view of his eyes, I take in their swirls of green and blue. Instead of a polite hello, I stumble over my words as he smiles so handsomely at me.

Off to a great start.

"Hello again, Ardella. I'm glad we ran into each other. Part of me wondered if I would," he tells me honestly in a low, arousing tone that pools in my belly like lava.

He's taller than me by at least eight inches. I keep that note in the back of my mind. Suddenly, it feels as if the library is too hot, and the space is so small.

"You too, Jack," I manage to finally reply.

Don't make a fool of yourself, Ardella.

He looks down at the books in his hands. "Interesting reads you have here... Where are you sitting? I'll carry them for you."

Offering a small smile, I incline my head, indicating for him to follow me. I lead him to my area for the day.

"I was reading about the afterlife, plus the varying beliefs people hold, and certain topics caught my interest more. A mere curiosity that needs to be satisfied," I tell him as he sets the books atop the others on the table next to my chair.

"My apologies, I wasn't judging you. I have odd reading interests, too. I was just amused by the topics that nearly dropped on me." His grin is cheeky as I wince in quick regret.

"I'm sorry about that. Are you injured?" I ask, giving him a once-over to make sure he isn't bleeding.

"Only a little," he says, lifting his hand up and pinching his fingers together to mimic his words.

Those eyes flash something hidden that I can't get a read on.

For once, I can't *read* someone. Maybe I'm off my game?

"What can I do to help...or make it up to you?" The words slip out without further thought, and I inwardly berate myself.

He could ask you for anything, Ardella.

The thrill of it courses through my body. Amusement dances in Jack's eyes as if he, too, knows he could rightfully ask anything of me.

I'm in shock yet again by his response. "Why don't we keep each other company today? I won't disturb you while you are reading, of course, unless you have a topic you are interested in discussing. I'll leave that up to your discretion."

I stare blatantly at his lips, wondering what they taste like before roving over his face to meet his eyes.

"Deal."

The corner of his mouth lifts as he excuses himself to find books.

Watching him move further away, I'm not subtle. I'm checking him out and liking what I see. Heat pools to my core again, and I shift, tugging my skirt down slightly to make sure I'm not blinding anyone. I adjust my knee-high socks before running a hand through my hair. I decide I look decent enough for the outing even if part of me holds doubt that I would be lucky enough to run into any of the two males.

What was the other guy's name in my room, anyway? I wonder if the two knew each other.

Let people look, though; who cares if my ass hangs out? Women should be able to wear what they want without judgment or fear.

The man wants to keep you company, Ardella.

Maybe I'll like him even further, enough that he'll take me behind the back shelves and slip those long fingers inside where I need them. Or he'll bend me over one of the tables and fuck me hard.

Biting my lip briefly, the thoughts are sinfully delicious as I pick up the book in my chair and continue reading, settling back in with my legs squeezing tight together.

Calm yourself, don't be an animal to the...delectable man. You don't know him; this isn't college!

Repeating it like a mantra, I quickly focus on the world around me as I continue reading about the afterlife, losing myself for the short remainder of its pages. When I finish, I glance up and realize Jack is sitting across from me reading. I grab the book about necromancy, swapping it with the one I just finished, but not before catching Jack's saccharine eyes.

A smile lingers on his lips while I settle back into the chair. I begin the book, reading about resurrection; I can feel those eyes remain on me.

No longer focusing on the book in my hands, I bite my lip gently, having yet another debate with myself. Do I flirt and see what happens, or do I pretend not to notice?

My core tells me she craves his attention, too.

Why are these strange men evoking such sumptuous lust?

I cross my legs coyly, looking up slowly to meet those darling eyes of his.

"How am I supposed to read with a focused audience?" I drop my tone, low and sultry.

His eyes match what I hope mine already convey.

Please, distract me, Jack.

"I'm in admiration of the sight. Does that bother you?"

Good call, Ardella. Keep it going. See how far he's willing to go.

"No. By all means...but," I pause and look off toward the window, then turn my head to the side, "you don't have to admire from afar. You can be closer."

His eyes narrow slightly as he calmly puts his book down next to him on the table.

"Come sit with me then. Let me read with you." His tone dips, and I can feel it in my pussy.

I smile sweetly, slowly closing my book, plus the finger I leave in it as I hold it in one hand. Uncrossing my legs and opening them slightly, I stand and make my way over to him.

He shifts his legs, and I can see his bulge as he pats his lap. His eyes are bright, the greens and blues swirling as he looks up at me, and I sit in his lap, adjusting to his arms gathering around me to help me hold the book.

Feeling hot and bothered, I take an easy breath, enjoying his warmth and his cock pressing against me. His woodsy scent engulfs me as he takes the initiative and places a kiss on my shoulder, where my sweater exposes my skin at the collar.

"I was at this particularly interesting section," I tell him quietly, leaning into him. "Let me know if I read too fast or slow. I'll wait for you."

He brushes the tip of his nose against my shoulder, lingering there as if battling with himself. *Such great battles, I couldn't wait to find out.*

I adjust myself slightly, feeling him tense and pulse against me. He whispers, "I will go at the pace you are accustomed to. Don't worry about me."

His breath is like feathers against my skin, eliciting goosebumps all down my body.

I begin to read, too distracted by him to read at my normal pace. My hands brush against his as we both hold the book together. The book isn't even heavy, but part of me feels that his hands would be all over me if he didn't hold the book. Not that I would tell him no, not when I craved his hand to glide under my skirt.

"Can you turn the page, please?" I ask him, soft and sweet. He flips the page, placing his chin on my shoulder. His face is near mine, so close I can feel his heat and follow his eyes as he reads the page. *So polite.*

With a smile, I tell him to turn the page again a minute later.

He does, and we continue for at least five minutes before the end of the chapter. Not that I have any clue what the words on the page are.

Instead of telling him to turn the page to continue, I slightly shift in his lap and turn my head to the side to find his eyes already on me. I melt into their depths as I lean closer, brushing my lips against his, waiting for him to decide whether to kiss me or not.

"You're playing a dangerous game, Ardella," his tone is low and deep as he speaks, and those words rush right to my pussy.

"What game is that, exactly?" I don't move, awaiting his next response.

"Do you think I'll stop at kissing you? I'm *barely* holding myself together now as it is."

Oh, *fuck.*

I'm sinfully wet. *We're on the same page.*

Holding his hand against the book in our grasp, I merge my lips with his. Undoing me at his softness, his words are magic to my flesh. Eager himself, he deepens the kiss immediately with a quiet groan. When he does it again, I take a risk, moving his hand under my skirt. He doesn't protest or move away and takes initiative. His hand moves higher up my thigh as mine rests on his arm, letting him explore.

Once he makes it to my underwear, he rubs where it's wet, a rumbling sound releasing quietly in his throat. Jack tugs on my bottom lip with his teeth.

"You're so fucking wet, Ardella."

I exhale lightly with a pleasured sigh as his fingers slip underneath to pet and stroke, enough so that I can feel my slickness against the crease.

I begin to capture his lips with mine once more, slipping my tongue inside; it muffles my soft moaning as he circles my clit with his thumb, two fingers slipping inside.

My hand fists the bottom of his shirt as his other cups the back of my head.

With my mind completely blank of all thoughts but him and a release I crave, his quiet noises bring me closer to the edge.

I open myself up more to him as he pumps his fingers faster, his thumb continues working my clit, swelling more under his touch. It amazes me how my body responds so immediately to his touch, and I dive straight into oblivion, crashing and falling as I ride out my release on his fingers with muffled sounds. My inner walls tighten on his fingers, a low growl vibrating through my mouth as we keep quiet, not wanting to draw unwanted attention. *As if I would care at that very moment.*

When my body relaxes, he pulls his slick fingers out, parting from my lips. I close my eyes and slowly open them to find him staring at me as he sticks those two fingers in his mouth.

"I'll save my tongue for next time, Ardella," he says to me after, and I feel hot again.

That was the sexiest thing anyone's ever done to me. The location certainly helps because who wouldn't want pleasure in their favorite place?

"And the time after that?" I ask, breathless.

"Lady's choice."

I kiss him, slowly meeting his blue and green eyes. "You have yourself a deal, Jack."

He relaxes as I lean into him fully, nuzzling my face into the crook of his neck. Jack holds me for a few minutes, and it's so damn blissful.

"Shall we grab some food and return to our books tomorrow?" He asks, and I nod, moving to stand up.

"I've been here all day; some food would be good. How do you know I'm free tomorrow?" I turn to him with the book in my hand. A charming look appears as he rises.

"I was hoping you would be."

At least he's honest, and I'm certainly eager too. "I am," I tell him sweetly.

He leans in to kiss me again before I gather my other books. "Let's leave the books at the front desk and tell them we'll be back tomorrow."

I agree, and we haul the stacks to the front.

The woman gives us an inquisitive look but settles on allowing us to keep them there until the following day.

"We promise to put them back in their respective places," Jack promises, and she bats her eyelashes at him, waving us out.

We are grinning as we leave the place, deciding to eat at the diner a few blocks away.

"Do you live nearby?" I dare to ask, and suddenly, he seems uncomfortable.

"Close enough, yes. My best friend lives with me; he's practically my brother, although not by blood. We grew up together."

Waiting for him to continue, he doesn't. I decide to say nothing else as we arrive at the diner. I don't want to intrude when he's already uneasy about the topic, tensing up beside me before gathering himself.

We seat ourselves, ordering water and a chicken dish for each of us. We chat idly over various books, and I begin to find Jack more comfortable to be around. It's easy to talk to him. He listens attentively, making eye contact and smiling or laughing whenever I say something flirty or funny. I hope he feels just as cozy with me, all the same.

The day went better than I originally expected. Jack even goes so far as to walk me home. I feel terrible about it, but he insists, trying to show me that not all chivalry is dead. It makes me giggle, but he kisses me once we're at my doorstep.

"See you tomorrow?" I offer.

"I'll be there," he promises.

I lean to kiss him again, and then he's off toward the darkness of the woods.

Once I make it inside, I peek through the blinds to find Jack lingering at the tree line before turning and disappearing in the dark from where we came.

I climb the stairs to my room in the memorized darkness.

There's a prickling sensation at the back of my head, a sudden reminder of an earlier time in my youth when I fell in love for the first time, only to have my heart ripped out, *twice*, by that person. The only difference is I'm not a teenager anymore.

I'm not who I was.

However, even if Jackson is delightful, I will not be so quick to give my heart away this time.

I refuse to be left behind again.

JACK — Past

Roman was right; not only was Ardella captivating in her beauty, but...those yellow eyes pierced through me. I wanted—*needed*—to see her again. According to him, she liked books, so part of me hoped I'd find her at the library. I'd leave the blatant stalking to him.

When I did go on the first sunny day after so much dreariness, I watched her from afar first, admiring that short fucking skirt covering just enough of her, but not enough at the same time. Transfixed on the bookworm that day... Was her skin as soft as it looked? Was she soft and delicate?

Just a taste. I needed a sliver.

There wasn't anything wrong with meek women or the opposite, but I had particular cravings. Docile wasn't a part of it. I enjoyed women with intellect and passion. Ardella brought out the fantasy. I couldn't get those eyes out of my mind.

It was adorable watching her linger upstairs as if she were a romance and flowers kind of gal, only to decide on her stack of books from the first floor. It was the ladder. The bookshelf ladder gets all the nerds at heart, including myself.

Once she was comfortable in her little reading spot by the window, I realized I could watch her for hours; no wonder Roman was obsessed. She looked so focused on reading, twirling her pale blonde hair between her fingers in concentration.

Although Roman made his bets, it really wasn't a contest. We were both curious about the yellow-eyed woman. *Ardella.* It was such a sensuous name, how it rolled off the tongue. *Mmm.*

The more I watched her, the more I wanted to find a backup option to the house robbery plan. I couldn't, in good conscience, rob her. Wouldn't put it past Roman, though. He was an ass.

I'd rather linger in the cemeteries and mausoleums or libraries. It was quieter there and held a dark beauty to it. But the home of where the dead were prepared? I didn't think I could go that far, even if I did find solace in the darker side of life.

Ardella was a mystery to me, one I needed to discover as if she were a fantasy book exploring new realms. And haunting in the sense of women who like the darker things that society turned their backs on, topics too taboo.

Many people were afraid of death, the fear of our mortality, or the emotions that crawled into the mind from funerals.

An existential crisis? No thanks.

When we robbed and temporarily tore up graves, I did my best to respect the dead, unlike my brother. Robbing them certainly *wasn't,* but I apologized to the person after covering their site back up with dirt, knowing they wouldn't need those valuable jewels in the afterlife; *hopefully not,* anyway.

I took great pride in making sure I left those gravesites as nice as I could, and I'd bring wildflowers and place them there; like a second apology would help.

Hours passed as my thoughts lingered on the fascinating woman tucked over by the large window. It was the same corner I liked to read in because of the location and natural lighting.

Great minds thought similarly, after all.

When Ardella emerged from her reading, I carefully placed my book back on the shelf, wandering to where she was leisurely. Focused and not paying attention to me, I knelt next to the ladder, pretending to search for books. My eye caught hints of her bare skin, and I could see right up her skirt. *Goddamn.*

Biting my lip, my mind jumped straight to the dirty, awful things I could see myself doing to her. Perhaps I would, if she let me. I wanted to take her knee-high socks off with my teeth and lick her from head to toe.

A book fell, followed by the rest. One hit me as I carefully stepped away; it was the universe's sign. *Stop being a pervert like Ro.*

Looking down at the books, I was most amused at her selections. *Witchcraft, the Light and Dark,* then *Necromancy Through the Centuries and Practices,* and a couple of books about cosmology and astronomy. My heart melted over it. Such peculiar reads, but so fascinating to me.

Keeping my humored expression, I picked them up and told her hello. She blushed and stared at me, her pupils adjusting, showing their desire and likeness. To distract myself, I offered to carry the books and teased her about being trampled by them. It was the *in* with her that I needed.

Ardella settled back into her spot as I excused myself to seriously search for books. I needed to tempt her to hang out with me more somehow. She looked like an angel bathed in light; a sense of mischief lingered in those yellow eyes. Damn, if she wasn't sexy before, it became more apparent while she sat reading with her thighs clenched together.

Wonder why that was?

Biting my lip at the sight, I found some classic literature books I had read before. Settling in across from her, I opened *The Count of Monte Cristo.* Pretending to read it, I eagerly watched her devouring whatever she read in her lap. Smirking to myself, I idly scanned a few pages before I snuck more glances, admiring how focused she was and the afternoon light hitting her just right.

After a bit, I caught her tugging on her lip.

How I wanted to tug on it, too.

When she finally flirted with me, I nearly lost it. The craving intensified as her desire danced in those stunning, captivating eyes. I could picture it as I told her to sit on my lap.

She would be bent over the chair, riding in my lap, or being displayed on one of the study tables after hours as I tasted her flesh. Such devious daydreams with swollen pink flesh as I consumed her cries of pleasure.

I was hard as a rock as she settled in. I didn't even hide it as I placed a kiss on her shoulder. She was radiating, and I can't say I complained about having her perched in my lap. It was strangely erotic as we read together, and she kept her cute little smile off and on, asking me to turn the page. I slowly scanned the words, and it was interesting enough but not enough to distract me from the lovely woman in my lap.

When Ardella finally shifted in my lap, I found myself staring at her intently, even more when she barely touched my lips with hers. I could nearly taste her, *so fucking close.*

Then, when she did kiss me, I groaned immediately. The taste of her was my undoing, with her lips molding to mine. Thus began my fantasy of having her lips wrapped around my cock; it was all I could think about while basking in her soft mewling sounds.

My mind drifted away, solely focused on her as I cupped her head, deepening our kiss. Ardella grabbed my other hand, moving it intentionally under her skirt. After fantasizing all day, *she* took the initiative. *Fuck me.*

I was hot all over, especially with how wet she was. It made me hungry, hungry to bury my face and taste the divine. However, for that round, I would let her guide the interaction, and it was a shock that she was more than willing.

Oh, my sweet, you're going to taste so exquisite when I defile you.

When she came apart, I put her back together again.

Ardella's muffled moans weren't enough for me, so I enticed her to continue and have dinner with me the next day after we ate at the diner, smiling like school children with secret crushes.

I adored those cute looks across the table as we ate, and then I paid and walked her home. I let my thoughts roam as I walked home, thinking over one of the best dates of my life with a charming yellow-eyed woman I couldn't get enough of.

Tomorrow couldn't come fast enough.

Once I made it home, Roman walked out of the bathroom in a towel. My smile never left my face as I took in his handsome sight. My depraved thoughts went to Ardella *and* him. How fucking perfect the three of us would be together.

Did I dare cross that line?

His questioning brown eyes pulled me out of such thoughts. "What are you smiling like an idiot for?" he piped up, a slow grin spreading from ear to ear.

"I had the most fascinating day at the library," I replied calmly, sitting on my bed from across the room.

He raised his brow, waiting for me to continue. I let him get fidgety as I took off my shoes.

"*Ardella.*" I knew the name would ring a bell.

He looked torn between jealousy and amusement. "I'm rather jealous of you, Jacky boy. *Do tell.*"

So, I did.

Both of us were salivating by the time I finished.

"I can't wait to taste her," he told me, and I agreed completely.

My finger tasting wasn't enough to hold me over. If anything, it tempted me further.

"Mind if I watch tomorrow? I'll stay hidden," he added suggestively with a wink as he threw on his pajama bottoms, moving to hang up his towel.

I considered his proposal and felt that familiar hunger travel straight to my chest, then my cock.

"Of course. I'll make sure to give you a good show," I teased as he laughed loudly, flopping on his bed.

"Why don't you show up to dinner at the diner and make yourself *known* tomorrow?"

"I will take you up on that. *One thousand times over.*"

With a grin, I moved to go get washed up. Tomorrow will be an exciting day for Roman *and* me.

I would taste her again.

It took everything in me to sleep that night.

PRESENT

Ardella wears a mid-length skirt the following day, appearing as beautiful as the day before. Her pale blonde hair is pulled back in a low ponytail, and she wears a white-knitted sweater that comes off her shoulders.

"Good morning," I tell her, and she brightens up, returning the greeting.

"I promise not to distract you too much today," I whisper at her side as we walk with our stack of books to a private table in the back, away from prying eyes.

We are nearly enclosed by walled bookshelves. It's perfect for what I plan for later with her spread out on the table. A perfect view for the handsome man that will be watching. I adjust myself over the thought as I sit at the table.

Ardella picks up the necromancy book from the prior day, briefly glancing at the stack I brought in.

"What are you reading?"

With a grin plastering my face, I flip the book in my hand over. "The book you were reading on the afterlife seemed interesting."

There's a whisper of a smile, amusement dancing in those eyes before she settles into reading.

Since yesterday, all I can think about is the taste that awaits me. However, it could wait until the afternoon. Sometimes, it's about the chase. I toss her a wink once her eyes meet mine briefly before focusing on our book reading.

After some time, I glance up and find her twirling her hair on her finger in concentration. A smile tugs as I move my leg under the table to touch the edge of hers.

I glance down back to my book when I feel her eyes on me while I keep rubbing my leg to hers.

There's a quick shuffle before I feel a foot instead of her leg.

The gesture is sweet, and we keep it casually going while continuing to read.

It isn't until I'm halfway through the book that I begin to

understand her fascination with certain topics. I find them appealing all the same.

There were different beliefs regarding the afterlife, depending on the culture. There was the Christian way, heaven—good, and hell—bad, amongst others, and there was the void of nothingness. There were philosophized views of multiple dimensions and rebirth through something new, which logically made sense to me.

Whether we are born as flies or a tree next, is the real question.

I can see how Ardella easily gets lost in it, especially yesterday. An educated woman with a mind of her own always draws me in. I crave to undress her, not only the woman but her mind. They both go hand-in-hand.

Society is slowly improving with women's rights, but it isn't where it needs to be either. There are still old ways of thinking that remain. Sometimes, it's all about power; other times, women aren't even respected. It's fucking foolish, if you ask me.

Why hold people to restrictions instead of letting them thrive?

By the time I finish the book, it's late afternoon, and Ardella is well into the book about witchcraft. Casually, I slide my leg between hers and rub my foot against hers to get her full attention.

Of course, let it be two bookworms to get distracted by *books*.

She looks up, awareness settling in those pale, yellow eyes. I hadn't realized how pale they looked yesterday. They are so much more intense now. I wonder if it's a mood situation or if her eyes do it naturally?

"Think you can spare some time?" My tone is low as she answers me by rubbing her leg against mine.

"Shall we return our finished books before we get a lecture from Suellen at the front desk?"

She huffs a laugh as we both stand, grabbing some books to put away.

I let her walk ahead of me, watching her hips sway with extra pizazz because she *knows* I'm looking. I smirk and catch my best friend on the other aisle, hidden away. We share brief gazes, and I wink at him before Ardella climbs the ladder.

Her ass is face level for me as I look around and hand her my book. She smiles down sweetly at me as I instinctively run my hand up the back of her thigh until I reach her ass.

She's *bare* underneath. *Naughty woman.*

Leaning into her, I release a low grunting noise as my finger slips between her lips, where I find her wet. My mind goes blank as I nip at her hip.

"I believe I was promised a tongue this time..."

She's biting her lip as I ease my finger out, squeezing her ass. "Gladly. *The coast is clear,*" I whisper as I help her down, and her eyes are a more vivid yellow.

Clasping her hand, I lead us back to our tucked away table. I move the books out of the way and spin around, pulling her into me and claiming those delectable lips. A cute little moan slips from her as I turn her around, nudging her to the edge of the table. I can see Roman peeking while pretending to look through a book.

Arms encircle around me, clutching me tight before cupping the back of my head to deepen the kiss. I'm nestled perfectly between her thighs while she wiggles her ass on the table.

"I can't wait to taste you," I murmur between kisses, letting my hands travel over her soft sweater back under her skirt. "Do you know how wet you are, Ardella?"

"I can't wait, either," she huffs, breathless from our ardent kissing.

"Show me," I breathe against her lips before licking them once.

Desire is all I can see shining in those yellow eyes. She immediately places my hands on her thighs, moving up her skirt. Those eyes watch me while laying herself back on the table. My prize is glistening as her thighs casually spread.

Am I dreaming?

"A most perfect feast," I praise, sneaking a glance to make sure Roman is watching before sinking down and wrapping my arms around her thighs as my hands rest on her abdomen.

Her pink lips are glistening, taunting me to come play. Kissing up her inner thighs, lightly nipping here and there, I lick up her labia, teasing her clit once before sinking my tongue into her wet cunt.

A low growl rumbles through me as I taste her essence, the dark woman that she is, along with those desires. She runs her hand through my hair, inspiring me further. Her quiet gasps are felt right down in my cock, aching to fill her. *That would have to wait.* I need her to come apart on my tongue first. There's a carnal desire to taste her cum; I will not settle until I have her all over my face.

Sucking her swollen clit, her hand tightens and pulls at my hair. Strangled moans of my own vibrate against her. Whenever I fuck her finally, it wouldn't be in the back of the library. *No,* it would be someplace where she could cry for me and scream at her leisure.

She writhes as I slip two fingers inside, stroking her and curling my fingers at the swell of her.

Roman is still holding a book, making sure no unwanted watchers come back to disturb us, and keeping those lustful eyes on the scene.

"Fuck," she manages to get out as her panting increases, and I bring my mouth back to the prize.

She tightens around my fingers, an oncoming shake while she grips the table. Glancing up briefly, her mouth parts, her eyes are closed, and her thighs then grip my head for dear life. Salivating over her taste, I make her ride out her release in full until she whimpers.

Goddamn, her pussy tastes fantastic.

It takes everything within me not to turn her over and fuck her on the very same table, yet I would keep it in the back of my mind for a later date.

I lap up every last drop of her, rising slowly after. I see Roman move slightly, and part of me wonders how hard he is right now.

I kiss her thigh and travel to her face and lips while I lean over the table. Pressing where I ache against her, she gasps while I help her sit up.

"Next sexual activity, *lady's choice,* although the desire to *fuck you right here* has never been stronger than it is after tasting *the afterlife* on these pretty pink lips." I nudge myself against her pussy to drive my point home.

She lowers her eyelashes, pressing her lips tight into a thin line before meeting my eyes.

"Not in the library, not where people can hear."

I can't help my look of mischief. "Exactly my point."

"Want to eat at the diner again?" She asks as if reading my mind.

I agree, and we leave the remaining books with Suellen again.

Roman is lingering nearby, making sure Ardella doesn't see him. I'm warm at the thought of him being with us all day. Just what doors would we unlock together?

"See you kids tomorrow," Suellen tells us with a shake of her head.

Reaching for Ardella's hand, I lace our fingers, happy that she accepted as we make our way over to the diner.

Part of me wonders when Roman will finally appear, but the diner doesn't look too busy yet, so our timing is good.

We sit in a back booth in a corner, and Ardella sighs quietly. "What's on your mind?" I ask after we order water.

Her eyes skim the menu, not quite answering me right away.

"Wishing we were somewhere else."

I flash her a knowing look, hinting at the same thing. "Me too," I whisper.

She catches my stare, and that's when I see him enter in all his glory.

Roman has the cockiest grin. The lust is still dancing in those eyes from the show earlier.

He appears at the side of the table. "Fancy seeing you here, brother." He winks at me before looking down at Ardella's scowl.

"You."

He slides into the seat beside her, and she rolls her eyes in disgust.

This will be interesting.

Humor fills me with the interaction as the server comes over to take our orders, and Roman orders a soda.

"Who's your friend, Jacky?" He looks between us both, pretending not to know.

Ardella looks like she wants to laugh over the nickname, and I don't miss her cute snicker over it.

"Ardella, this is Roman," I introduce, seeing her throw Roman a look of warning.

"Lovely name for a lovely woman," he says with a familiar allure when he's charming someone. "Why the face, doll?"

"Oh, I don't know. Maybe because I first met you in the *dark of my bedroom! Weirdo.*"

He grins unabashedly. "Oh, you don't even *know* the half of it, sweetheart."

Although she seems bothered by his presence, her eyes are still yellow and bright. She enjoys the banter. I wouldn't point it out to her in front of him, though.

"Are you the only one in the family with those eyes, Arde?" Roman asks, leaning closer as she swats at him.

A deep chuckle of amusement left his pretty lips.

"Don't *ever* call me that again, especially if *you* want to keep your balls."

His mouth falls open in false shock as I hide my smirk.

Pointing at her and looking at me, he grins. "Does she talk to you like that?"

I shake my head, and my hands shoot up in quick defeat. "I wasn't in her bedroom *uninvited.*"

"That's a shame," is all he says as Ardella hides her smile. The food is then brought out, pausing the conversation.

I make simple small talk with Roman while Ardella eats in silence, trying to gauge the situation or how to act around us both, I'm sure. First meetings can be uncomfortable for anyone.

"Does being around dead people bother you?" Ro randomly says once we finish dinner and order milkshakes.

"No. The dead are at least quiet, *unlike you.*"

He pretends to be wounded. "What? I'm quiet, right, Jacky boy?"

Ardella doesn't suppress her giggle when I make a face.

Shaking my head, I say, "Don't lie, you are *not* quiet. You're loud."

"I see how it is," he fake pouts, and I find the whole interaction wholesome.

Our milkshakes come minutes later, and I pay for all of us so the server can attend to the growing customer crowd.

We all join in conversation, making small talk to help Ardella get more comfortable around Ro. Not that he makes it easy with his teasing demeanor.

"Want to take a relaxing stroll through a cemetery on the walk back to your house?" I offer, and she nods immediately.

My morbid angel.

We leave once we finish our milkshakes, walking the Morella town streets with their old styled lamps and cobblestone sidewalks until we reach the forest tree line.

"I don't know why I hang out with such weird people." I roll my eyes at Roman's remark.

"Then don't come," Ardella tells him simply.

He nonchalantly slides his arm around her shoulder. "And miss the opportunity to annoy you? *Never.*"

"Ughhh," she shrugs him off as he laughs, clearly enjoying how he rubs her the wrong way.

Or is it secretly the right way?

Hopefully, it changes. *Even if he does make it harder on himself.*

We stroll through the small cemetery as Roman eases into her side.

"You and I are going to have so much fun, Arde," he mentions as her look changes from disgust to sudden intrigue.

"Call me that again, I dare you," she taunts, and like a fool, Ro falls for it.

I'm in the middle of them, seeing my brother take the bait. *So, I move.*

"Arde," he says, and she's on him at once.

She has him by the balls and begins to twist, and he succumbs to her so easily.

"Hey, hey! Okay! Sheesh!"

The sight is unbearably sexy, and the proud look she wears afterward as he holds his junk, scowling that she got him good.

Laughing to myself, I pull a grinning Ardella to my side and walk with my arm around her, leaving the cemetery.

"Feel free to put him in his place anytime," I say softly into her ear.

"I will, most definitely." She turns her head to the side to give me a big smile.

"The people in my life are conspiring against me," I hear Ro say from behind us while we continue through the woods with the crunch of the fall leaves under us. "Damn woman, you've got a grip. Did you have to squeeze so hard? How am I supposed to fuck or jack off?"

I snort, and Ardella pipes up. "Not my problem. Learn to listen when a woman tells you something instead of being an asshole."

He doesn't say anything else afterward. The moon lights up the sky as we continue in silence. Eventually, she thanks me for dinner, and Roman is still groaning.

"Fuck, did she get you that good?" I turn to find him hunched over a couple of feet away.

"Yes."

"I'll get him some ice. We're almost there, let's go," she compromises as I sigh, and my brother shoots me a glance.

You deserved it, Ro, don't give me that look. We're not robbing her either.

We make it within ten minutes, and she takes us up to her room. *Willingly, this time.*

"This is how you're supposed to be in a lady's room—when

she *invites* you," she tells him, pointing to her bed for him to lie on.

I sit in a chair nearby, watching him obey with delight.

She really does have him by the balls, even still.

"I'll be back. Behave," she motions to him, more so than me.

We exchange smiles before she closes the door behind her to grab ice.

"You going to make it?" I dare to ask him.

"I was only teasing her."

"Yeah, don't think you were on the level to do that with her yet. You should've dialed back, but too late now."

He grunts, saying little else until she comes back.

She slowly makes her way to the side of the bed, looking down at him. "Sorry for hurting you. *Even if you did deserve it.*"

"I'm sorry, too, for being in here before and for terrible first impressions."

She offers him a half smile before she takes the bag of ice and climbs over him.

The sight of it goes straight to my groin. It shouldn't have, but weird fantasies come to mind. *I'd watch them, too.*

Ardella straddles his thighs and hands him the bag.

"What are you doing?" He asks, the pitch rising in his voice as she tugs his pants down, leaving his boxers still up.

Ignoring him, she reaches her hand out, indicating for him to give her the ice bag.

His breath hitches loudly, cursing when she places it right on his balls.

"Such a baby," she tells him, and I can't help but snicker.

"Quiet, you. Your balls weren't grabbed and twisted," he directs toward me.

"In her defense, she warned you, asshole." He groans in defeat.

"Thanks, Jackson," she says while looking down at Roman, leaning closer to his face.

"Can't believe you two are related. One is less annoying than the other."

"It's part of my charm. The women love it," he comes back with, and sadly, he is right; they *do* like it.

Ardella isn't like most women, though, and I fancy that about her *a lot*.

"I find that hard to believe. Not all women are the same, you know."

They stare at each other.

"Allow me to make it up to you then." I see his eyes roving over her perfect face.

I watch them in amusement as she shakes her head. "Not necessary."

"I insist," he counters back.

She lets her lips graze his, making him think she's going to kiss him.

Shifting her position, he moves slightly and her hand is back down holding the ice firmly to him.

Her lips move away.

"Hold still," she orders as he wiggles under her.

"It's *cold,*" he whines.

"My God, you are a petulant child!"

He narrows his eyes, opening his mouth to say something, but quickly decides to shut up with whatever look she gives him.

Finding them adorable, I ruminate on how we would be just fine in the end.

Part of me thinks Ardella secretly enjoys the banter with Ro.

"*Tease,*" is all I hear him say.

"Another five minutes, and you should be fine. If not, take the ice with you."

He is silent for a minute before asking her. "You never answered my question earlier. Are you the only one in your family with yellow eyes?"

She nods. "Yes. Why do you ask?"

His brown eyes lock on hers. "I've never seen anything like it. They're captivating."

"Thanks...I guess. Don't think that compliment lets you off the hook completely. I'll let you live another day."

He raises his brow. "Oh, really?"

"Did you think growing up in a mortician's home that a lady wouldn't know how to kill a man several different ways and destroy a body so it's never found? *Please.*"

My brother and I gulp, but strangely I find the statement sexy.

What is wrong with me?

"Noted. I wave my white flag."

She laughs genuinely, climbing off him, and getting out of bed.

"Feeling better?" She asks as he sits up and nods.

"I'll take the ice with me to be sure." He pulls up his pants while moving to stand fully.

I take it as my sign to rise and move towards the exit with my brother.

"Tomorrow?" I ask over my shoulder to Ardella, letting us lead the way to her front door.

She inclines her head to me, kissing my cheek in farewell once we're there.

I open the door, stepping out into the crisp night. "Until next time, Yellow Eyes."

"Bye," is all she tells Roman.

I give her a wave while we walk away from the house, disappearing amidst the trees.

"That went well," he says.

"Did you have to bug her like that?" I question, wondering when he'll behave for once in his life.

He puffs out a breath. "I can't help it sometimes, you know me... But goddamn, the sight at the library. How did she taste?"

I stare at him with my most impish smile. "Like a fucking dream."

"Knew it."

"If you play your cards right, Ro, perhaps you'll win her over eventually."

"I plan on it," he promises. "Maybe."

Once we are further away, I dare to voice my house robbing hesitancy. "I don't think we should rob her house anymore. I can't do it in good conscience. Maybe we should ask for her help? She's understanding. And smart as hell."

"We're so close, Jackson, so close to freedom I can taste it," he insists.

"It's not the end of the world. It's also not fair to Ardella to ever feel used like that. I refuse to do it," I counter back immediately.

"Her pussy was that good, huh?" I shoot him a daring look. "Okay, fine. We'll figure out a new plan. Maybe we'll get lucky grave digging and hope for the best."

He sighs in defeat as I pat his back while we make our way home.

Eternally, I'm grateful that Ardella is a dream made a reality, and I think she secretly enjoys Roman's teasing.

Too soon to tell, though.

E.G. POA

CHAPTER TEN

MY LITTLE RAVEN

ARDELLA

Slowly, over the following weeks, I begin to find Roman less troublesome between helping my dad with a few services and reading sessions with Jack. Maybe I have been denying myself, but I *enjoy* the banter with Roman. Seeing the two men together makes me warm and hot, and it isn't just Jackson I'm picturing filling me up.

When I initially met Roman, I could see a lingering darkness in those eyes of his, disguised under his humor and smart mouth. A part of him that he hid away, probably for fear of abandonment; no wonder he was an ass. Yet, that same darkness called to my own.

These men can give me what I want, and it's wonderful to be craved by them equally.

I can see the all too familiar gaze settling in Roman's brown eyes. I can envision running my fingers through his dark hair and yanking it as he brings me over the edge. Maybe it would finally shut his smartass mouth up.

The two men aside, my sister, Kenzie, finally makes an appearance.

She's looking unwell and mostly ignores me when I try to make small talk. She hides in her room when she isn't assisting our father. Reynolds shows up, too. Oddly enough, the whole family is under one roof. I can't remember the last time we were under one roof longer than a single night. Although Kenzie isn't talkative with me, Reyn isn't either which is odd.

A sense of dread fills me, giving me an aura of foreboding that I can't explain. Not only is my archnemesis spreading lies and slander about some recent critiques, but my father is looking worse for wear.

Was something happening around me that I wasn't paying attention to? Were there signs I was missing?

I think back to our last conversation as I walk through the woods, nearing one of the cemeteries that's a thirty minute walk from home.

"Dad, is everything okay? You don't seem like yourself," I paused, waiting for him to meet my gaze. "Anything I can do to help?"

We had been gathering up the flowers to send to the mourning family to be picked up by one of the flower companies that delivered them to their door.

"All will be fine, Ella. Soon, everything will be right again."

I tilted my head, fear pulsing through my chest as I became frantic before he enveloped me in his arms, petting my hair. Somehow, the gesture made me forget.

"There is nothing to worry about, my sweet girl. An old man's woes have nothing to do with yours. Keep those men in line, alright?"

I laughed bitterly, wondering why it felt like he was saying goodbye. And for what? What secrets did he keep?

Tears glisten in my eyes as I blink them away at the memory of what my father's possibly hiding...

I'm nearing the sacred ground of the dead. Yet, instead of being alone, I find two men digging up the same body put in the ground two days prior. Wondering what the men are up to, I close the door of my fear lingering thoughts.

Remaining hidden in the shadows, I lean on a large statue nearby, trying to listen.

"Do you have the stuff?" A deep voice asks, and my skin prickles.

Why does that voice sound familiar?

They have to be some criminal grave robbers, so desperate for money they need to *rob the dead.*

I'm not sure who I feel worse for, the men stealing or the deceased person.

These buffoons have no respect!

The dead need to rest in *peace* and be left alone. Did they not think that some spirits would be restless or vengeful?

Not these guys... *Evidently.*

"Yeah, yeah, I got them! I think this will be enough for us. We'll be free of that place, Jacky."

Wait a goddamn minute.

I step out of the shadows, unseen to the men. The grave robbers are Jack and Roman.

What the fuck?

Leaning against the statue, I wait, fuming and crossing my arms over my chest with a frown while watching Jack help Roman out of the plot hole.

"Grave robbing from the dead for sport is what you both do in your spare time. Interesting."

They jump out of their skin, cursing loudly. Clearly, *I* spooked them.

Good, let them be worried.

I've caught them doing something so taboo even *I* don't know what to think. Death is already a topic that makes people uncomfortable, but robbing someone not even alive to defend themselves? I can't figure out how to feel.

"Jesus fucking Christ, Arde, don't ever do that again!" It's Roman who speaks first.

"What are you doing here, Ardella?" Jack asks next, hesitant to step in my direction as he holds the shovel in one hand before shoving it into the ground.

"What? Cat got your tongue because you're caught in the act?" I raise my brow as they run their hands through their hair with worry.

"Look, it's not what it looks like," Jack begins, and Roman throws his hands up sarcastically, scoffing.

"Oh, that's fucking clever, Jackson. Don't lie to her when it's exactly what it fucking looks like!"

I nearly smile at Roman's comment but keep my face neutral. I'm disappointed, no matter what my attraction is toward them.

"Okay, fine." Jack slouches in defeat, rubbing between his eyes, clearly trying to talk his way out of it.

Once I realize they won't hurt me for catching them in the act, I move closer, hearing Roman mumble obscenities to himself and Jack watching me closely.

"So, tell me, what's so important for you to resort to this?" I question them while pointing my hand to the hole before me.

I move to the next tombstone and mutter a quiet apology to its owner as I sit on the flat surface at the top. Crossing my arms once more, I wait expectantly for their response.

The two men look at one another, having some sort of silent discussion; Roman steps closer first.

"You see, Yellow Eyes..." He sighs again, fidgeting with his hands.

Roman, *nervous? This keeps getting better and better.*

I find in that moment how I enjoy seeing him squirm. Hiding my smirk, I make a motion with my hand for him to spit it out already.

"So, Jacky and I grew up in town, right, and still live in the boy's home we grew up in... We'll save the tragic backstories for another time... We are adults now and have to resort to night-walker activities to get by, err, *out* of there rather."

My heart plummets into the hole they had dug. *Wonder what kind of tragedies?*

"Jack and I are like family, although not related. We had been doing these nefarious deeds to get out of there. *That* place is our shame and our sanctuary from all the hurt and pain we endured. It's not what you want to hear, but it's the truth. We did what we needed to survive, and with these trinkets and treasures these dead people aren't using, it'll go towards something *good*. That's how *I* look at it. We don't have to like it either, but you asked. I will not apologize for what we need to do or how. *As if you didn't already hate me enough...*" His downcast look at the ground has him moving a foot closer to me as Jack leans on the shovel, still in the ground, lost in thought.

"I don't hate you, Roman," I say quietly once he's in front of me, and in the light of the lanterns they brought with them, his dark eyes lock intently onto my own.

"While I appreciate that sentiment, my little raven," he exhales, leaning closer to gaze upon my face, "what are you going to do with this information now?"

"Is there a following threat if I don't keep this quiet?" I dare to ask in a low, uncertain tone.

His closeness makes me unfurl my arms to grip the stone to keep from kissing him. *Something I've thought about doing for over two weeks.*

I didn't ask too many questions about their past because I could see darkness lingering in their eyes, plus they kept their answers short.

Maybe someday they will trust me enough with their truths. As much as I banter with Roman, he doesn't deserve whatever it is he runs from or avoids speaking about.

Tonight's a start.

"Maybe," he whispers as his lips brush against mine, steadying his hands on either side of me, barely touching my hands on the tombstone.

My breath holds tight as his lips hover still. *This must be payback for teasing him on my bed.*

"I'm not judging you for how you choose to survive, just...*please* be respectful of the dead," I tell him, nearly breathless, and he hasn't even kissed me yet.

Warm air leaves his mouth, sweeping across my face as he leans back with a small smile.

He wanted a reaction out of me, and I gave it to him like an *idiot.*

"We are careful, and Jacky puts things exactly as we find them, right, Jackson?" He turns toward his brother, who nods quickly in agreement before returning those dark eyes to me.

"I'm not a snitch. What do I have to gain from it?" I say honestly.

He considers me. "I don't know, Little Raven of Death, you are '*tapping at my chamber door*'."

Before I can roll my eyes, his soft lips meet mine. My heart begins to sing over the gesture. Roman pulls away with that devilish smirk, full of secrets and hidden promises—ones unknown to me, *for now.*

"Will you keep us company, then?" He asks, moving further away.

My mind focuses on how his lips are softer than I imagined and how I'm left feeling dazed yet craving more. A strange desire washes over me as I stare at him. He *has* to know what he's doing to me; I can almost taste it.

"Of course. Show me how criminals live."

He chortles, and Jack breaks out into shy, uncertain laughter with him. The sound brings a satisfied smile to my face, breaking any earlier tension.

I watch Jack move the dirt back into the ground.

"Aren't you going to help him?" I ask expectantly of Roman. "He does it better; normally, I'd be gone making sure the goods are safe by now."

I roll my eyes, chiding him. "How *polite* of you."

Jack still has a couple of hours at best, even with his strength. He also seems to be moving slower with me there, so I come up with an idea then.

"Well, *show* me then. Afterwards, *you* can walk me home."

Roman seems intrigued by the thought before speaking over his shoulder while keeping his amusement. "That alright with you, Jacky?"

"Go for it. I work faster alone, anyway."

I hop off the tombstone, watching those dark pools follow me as I walk to Jack. The man himself pauses with a look of concern.

Once I'm close and personal, I kiss him sweetly with affection. "You can trust me. I will not say anything. Both of you deserve to live the life you crave."

He relaxes instantly, returning the kiss before tucking a strand of hair behind my ear. The gesture is sweet as I give him a reassuring smile while he says his thanks.

Leaving the man to work without distraction, I follow Roman through the cemetery. He pats his pouch on his hip when I shoot him an expectant look. He shrugs as we make our way through the woods. The air is slightly chill while we remain side-by-side.

"Do you always wander out late at night?" He asks out of nowhere several minutes later.

"Sometimes... I need extra quiet, or I want to bathe in natural water. Depends on my mood and need to escape," I answer truthfully, not caring that he knew one of my secrets of bathing outdoors at night.

"Graveyards are comforting to you?"

His eyes find mine as he moves his head to the side, dark hair falling into his face slightly.

I nod in confirmation. "*Cemeteries*—graveyards are connected to churches, technically."

Half a grin appears. "Jack's right, you are a *morbid* angel." "I'll take it as a compliment," I respond simply, wondering if he meant it that way or if he is still figuring it out.

"Since you were spying on us, how would you feel to know *I* spied on *you?*"

My brow rises high, pursing my lips while he slows beside me. Tilting my head, I dare to ask. "Are you telling me *you're* a stalker?"

"Yes."

Roman's face doesn't waver from what I can see in the darkness. Hiding my delight, I find it more intriguing than anything. Not that I would tell him that. It may have initially bothered me when I caught them in the cemetery, but when he explained, all I could do was sigh in defeat. They just want a better life, by whatever strange, taboo means necessary. Who am I to judge them?

I must be as sick as Roman to be intrigued by stalking. Madness calls to others' madness—it just occurs on different levels. *Wonder if it was my house or out here in the trees?*

"Where, then?" I question him, beginning to take a step forward when he stops altogether.

"You really want to know?" I turn myself to the side, letting my eyes adjust more to the nighttime dark.

"Before we ever met, we originally planned on robbing your house... I thought that if such a large home housed the preparation of the dead and that sort—it would be easy money."

Placing my hands on my hips, I say, "And who's the morbid one again?"

He continues on, ignoring me. "After another dig night, I made my way through the woods and accidentally found you bathing... I followed you home, realizing where you lived. Jack and I came up with a plan once we read in the paper of the viewing from the girl that died in her sleep."

"The heart attack... Of course." My arms fall back to my side as I exhale a heavy breath.

I catch the look he gives me, enough features to get his knowing expression across. "Yes, I was sneaking around your house when you caught me. I wasn't truly in the dark the entire time. Your room smelled good, and my mind wandered about the pale haired woman I found bathing. I couldn't help myself..."

"So, a set up distraction, sniffing—wait, how did you know it was my room?"

He steps toward me and leans closer. "You walked by, and I smelled your scent as you were wandering around the crowd. Also, the *vibes*."

"Okay..." I blink, realizing how close he is yet again. "Did you take anything?"

"Other than my imagination, no."

A half laugh leaves my throat, partially in disbelief over the man in front of me.

"Imagination of me naked aside... What else?" I keep my chin up, staring him down, ignoring the wetness gathering between my thighs over how much I delight in his unveiling truths.

"Well, Jack told me about meeting you at the library, and I decided to indirectly join."

I freeze, narrowing my eyes at what he's implying.

"You saw us—*me.*" It wasn't a question, but I couldn't deny the heat pooling within, traveling and spreading like a bitch in heat.

"I did." *That fucking grin again.*

I swallow, taking a breath. Roman leans closer to me, rubbing his nose against the corner of my mouth. I keep my hands tight at my side, resisting the urge to grab him.

"And what a sight it was." He presses his cheek against mine as if resisting too. "It took everything within me not to interrupt and join in. I almost pleasured myself at the sexy sight of you coming and your swollen lips while he licked you good... Christ, it was all I could think about."

When he lifts his face away from mine, I stare up at him defiantly.

"I also needed to make sure no one else got to see the show. It was a one person viewing only."

It's fucked up and twisted, and I love every minute of his confession. Having been watched is enticing to me now that I know...*my fantasies can carry me.*

"So, you watched from the sidelines. Why didn't you come up to me in the woods like the creep you are?"

He quickly walks me backward until I'm being pressed against the tree while we hold intense gazes. A predatory stare at that, one I enjoy from him and Jack alone.

"I told myself I *would* do it the next time I saw you. As fucked up as I am, Arde, I wouldn't have approached that first night. Jack is more charming than me. I know I'm rough around the edges and probably undeserving of any attention you would ever give me, if at all. I saw you smile that first night at the diner and come apart on my best friend's tongue, and goddammit, did I want to at least try—for *you*."

His head is now beside mine, speaking low in my ear as he presses hard against me. A war erupts within me on how I want to act in return.

Would Jack be mad?

I haven't fully fucked him yet, but I don't want to be inconsiderate.

"What does Jack think about that?"

"It's a sexy pissing contest at this point, my little raven." Well, *shit*.

"What if I tell you I plan to bathe in the woods tomorrow night? *What then?*" My breath comes out uneven and shallow while my heart thrums in excitement.

"You better hope I'm not busy because the water is big enough for two..."

God, I wanted him to reach under my dress and have him feel what he was doing to me.

"Tell me, little raven, are you wet between your thighs? Are you fucked up too?" His nose nuzzles my cheek before dipping to my neck and breathing deeply.

"*Yes,*" I want to say.

Instead, I ruin the moment, fucking with us both. "Don't you have precious jewels to take back to wherever? Mr. Criminal."

His laughter tickles my ear, kissing my cheek.

"Indeed," he says with a sigh, and I can hear the hint of disappointment laced in it.

Me, too.

He grabs my hand, distracting me from my lustful thoughts while I curse myself for not letting him find out. *Let me see if he shows up the following night.*

To my surprise, he brings me into town right in front of a dilapidated building. It looks abandoned and falling apart. Did they genuinely live here?

He ignores my look of shock, telling me to wait and that he will be right back. I wait reluctantly in the shadows, worrying over them and wondering if they need more ways to make money to get out of this place. It doesn't look safe to live in. It could crumble at any moment. From what I can see the roof is still intact.

I shouldn't feel as protective as I do, but the two men are growing on me quickly. More than I care to admit—at least for Roman, but I'm beginning to see beneath the exterior he put on.

"Ready?" He asks out of nowhere, making me jump before lacing our fingers and pulling me away from the building that should probably be torn down.

It seems as if he doesn't want me there from what I piece together by nonverbal cues as we walk fast back toward the woods.

"Do you not want me to see where you live?" I manage to ask later, after processing; my heart is in my throat.

"No. Don't say anything else. It's a shame I carry."

"You can't help it—" He stops suddenly, forcing me to turn around before lips claim mine possessively, stealing my breath away.

I can't hide my moan as his grip tightens at my hips.

"That's enough talk about that decrepit place. *Fuck.* I can't wait to see what sounds I can bring from those lips..." He kisses me hard again, and my arms draw up around him.

Licking my bottom lip as if asking for permission, I groan and let him explore, swirling in a new torturous dance.

I lose track of time, basking at the taste of him, and his eagerness.

"I'll kiss you all night at this rate..." Roman is the first to break the kissing session.

My hand is under his shirt, tracing shapes of familiar tombstones of my youth while he tugs on my lip with his teeth.

"I hope you bathe in the moonlight again tomorrow." I lean into him, licking his mouth to tease him. "Guess you'll find out," I croon coyly.

I can make out his devilish smile in the dark, and we continue the journey back to my house.

A huge part of me hopes he will show up since my pussy craves it–*him*—and perhaps the rest of me does too.

CHAPTER ELEVEN

IT IS HER AND I

ROMAN

I stand under the familiar trees, waiting in the shadows until she arrives. Part of me holds some doubt, but as always, she continues to surprise me. The air is too crisp to be swimming, but I refuse to let such an opportunity pass me by. My Little Raven is an enchantress in her death service place.

Watching from beside the large tree, Ardella strips down until she's bare. The moonlight kisses her skin so softly, so elegant and pale, like death itself. I wait with bated breath for a short while until I make myself known. I didn't tell Jackson where I'd be. Tonight is about her and me, where I met her first. Somehow, I knew I'd find myself back here.

"Bathing alone at night is certain to attract predators... Are you not afraid?" My tone is low, my need to take her forcing its way down to my cock.

A pale head of hair peeks from the water like a siren. Her ears are above it, so I know she hears me as I inch closer. My

Little Raven stands more, exposing her breasts, those yellow eyes watching me with interest. Nearly drooling over such a sight, her flesh begs to be worshiped amongst the trees at the water's edge.

"No... Should I be?" Her sultry tone reels me in, completely under her spell.

Her death siren call. "Maybe. Can I join you?"

"There's room for two," she says in a low, purring tone that entices me.

Taking off my clothes slowly, her eyes stay on me the entire time, and it's positively thrilling. With the way her yellow eyes twinkle under the moonlight, I begin to wonder who the true predator is.

I stand before her, exposed and highly erect, watching her eyes focus on me as I make my way toward her.

You will be able to taste me soon, little raven.

"Did I tell you how riveting you are?" I inquire as she submerges herself, keeping those eyes locked on me.

I'm finding how much I adore her attention, especially when she sasses me back.

"No. Why don't you tell me once more?"

"You," I say once I'm in front of her, "are," dropping my head to her ear to whisper, "riveting."

I hear her breathing along with a humming noise in her throat. "Are you my predator, Roman?" She asks quietly, glancing up at me with brighter yellow eyes, the true predator of these woods.

"Yes," I tell her honestly.

"Consider me captured," she murmurs right before claiming my lips.

I pull her in close, my hands dropping to her hips as she tugs on my bottom lip, her hunger feeding mine.

"It's a strong tie between being sweet or fucking you as you deserve, My Little Raven."

Her mouth is agape when she pulls away. I stick my thumb in it, holding her chin as she sucks it slowly, wrapping her soft tongue against my rough skin.

The gesture makes me envision those lips and tongue wrapping around my cock as I fuck her mouth. I grow more at the thought, beginning to throb over the fantasy, but not for much longer. I nudge it against her, and she releases my thumb with a small gasp.

"Turn around, Yellow Eyes."

She groans as I hug her close to me, placing my cock between the apex of her thighs to tease her.

Continuing to do so, my hands roam, cupping her ass and appreciating how it fits in my palm so nicely. I knead her breasts next, placing gentle kisses on her neck and shoulder. She moves her hair out of the way for me, pushing her hips back to give friction on my cock. We are beginning a new sexual dance between us, the tension over the last few weeks leading to this moment with her.

A growl rumbles from me as she leans into me all the same. "Tell me what you want, little raven. Do you want me to fuck your mouth or another hole of your choosing?" "Fuck," she curses, reaching behind to grab my ass.

My Little Raven is dizzy with lust, and I adore it. We're only getting started.

I tuck her earlobe between my teeth, enjoying the display and desire.

Was my raven as ravenous as me?

"Fuck my mouth. Let me taste you," she demands desperately, and I pull her further so she can kneel in the water and suck my cock while still being able to breathe.

Once she's at my feet, I brush my fingers gently across her

cheek. Those needy eyes kill me on the spot.

"He's all yours tonight. Go on, have a taste," I encourage. She's my reaper, and I'm ready to be taken home.

Using her mouth and hand, her lips enclose my tip, licking and sucking until I shiver.

"I want to hear you gag," I say as she removes her hand without a word.

Taking a fistful of her hair, I slowly inch in further until I hit the back of her throat. She gags as I expect, and I proceed to fuck her mouth.

"Breathe through your nose, little one. Enjoy the result of me coming apart because of you and what you do to me. *My Little Raven.*"

Humming on my cock, I observe her as she takes all of me while I fuck her mouth. I begin panting rapidly, feeling the rise within. She has her eyes closed with muffled sounds as she drools all over me.

"You're a dream come true with how well you take me. It has been all I've thought about since you sassed me. These lips, this night, and you bare before me."

Her eyes shoot open, looking up between her lashes. Fantasy turns into reality *finally*.

I jerk and jolt at the sensations exploding through me, stiffening while I shoot cum down her throat. I curse when I see how she drinks down every last drop.

Fuck.

Releasing my hold on her, I help her toward the bank.

Laying flat with my feet in the water, I instruct her, "Now, sit and let me eat. Let me worship you."

She licks her lips and carefully positions herself above my face, thighs on either side of my head. Mesmerized by the sight of her pussy, I glance up to find her watching me.

Grabbing her ass, I move her closer to my mouth. "There,

that's better," I speak, before claiming a taste. Jackson is right; she tastes divine.

I lick her swollen mound, moving from her clit to her entrance.

After watching Jack enjoy himself and bragging about how lovely she tasted, I'm more than eager to have her coming apart in my mouth as I lap at her pussy. To my delight, it's not long before her hands dive into my hair, fucking my face.

Reveling in it, she's taking what she needs from me. I can't get enough of it, *of her*. I've been dreaming of her since I saw her here all those weeks ago, and to finally have her...I'm not sure I'll be able to walk away after this.

Growling into her wet slit, I make her come for the first time with just my tongue. When she shakes, I keep going, her whimpers turning into loud cries as I adjust my hold to slip my finger inside, then slowly add another.

God, she's so tight.

"I love the way you fuck my face," I huff out as I switch fingers, using my thumb and my pointer finger to tease her sensitive clit.

Hovering over my chest, I use my other hand to grab one of her breasts, kneading and teasing her peaks. Moans of beauty fill me and the air around us as she cries out with a curse.

Pumping faster, I curl my thumb, stroking her deeper. Her walls are soon clamping down as she shatters more harshly the second time, nearly screaming. Squeezing her breast in hand, her head tilts back, riding it out entirely.

"So fucking beautiful," I say to her.

It's encouraging me as I quickly move my hands and lift her ass before getting up myself. Scooping her up swiftly, she squeaks out in surprise as I ease us back into the cool water. Initially, it's shocking, but not deterring, not when her hungry eyes are narrowing in on me.

Quickly adjusting to the water and the warmth of her, those arms wrap around me, then her legs. A harsh kiss meets my lips, our needs mirroring one another.

Ardella holds me with a sense of desperation and urgency with her tongue seeking out mine.

I accept, tasting myself on her tongue. My cock begins to thicken once more, somehow adjusting to the cold temperature.

"Take me, Roman. Fuck me as I deserve."

As if she answers my unsaid prayers, I do as she requests, gripping her ass to guide myself inside.

No longer is there concern with the water or anything else. I ease in slowly at first, letting her adjust, before fully seating myself.

Her nails dig into me as she holds on tight while I guide the thrusts, the weight of the water assisting us both.

Ardella is so perfectly wrapped around me, *so good* at claiming me as she does. My sensuous lover, my sanctimonious little raven.

Squeezing me as I push and pull, I prolong this bliss for as long as possible to savor being buried deep.

"You taste and feel exactly as I imagined."

Her hand dives into my hair as she gets out breathlessly, "Describe it to me."

"You are such deadly perfection. Soft and morbid in your beauty. That smart mouth, so smart that I eat up every last word. Lips that suck my cock so, as if you were made to claim me. Your touch is my afterlife, My Little Raven. I am already addicted to how we claim one another. Don't think I'm done with you after this."

A torturing moan slips out of those pale lips as I slam back inside.

"Cry for me, baby. Let me hear you. Milk my cock for all I'm worth."

Continuing my savagery at how I'm fucking her, Ardella cries for me, strangling my cock as a rumble tears through me with my release.

I'm practically seeing stars with how hard I come, and we hold each other tight, cursing under our breaths before laughing, leaning our foreheads together.

"I am definitely your stalker," I admit while we pant in the aftermath of claiming each other.

Someday, I hope to capture her heart, too.

Kissing her once more, she drops her legs down and pulls me under.

In the darkness is her and I, a quiet world, blissful without sound. Bubbles that remind me I'm alive and hopelessly in love with the yellow-eyed lover who found me in the dark.

I have drifted there for so long, life feeling meaningless. Where there was nothing, a seed sprouted within my chest, one that she planted.

A casket of seductive death with her pale beauty and haunting eyes. All feels right again. *She* feels right like I finally belong somewhere after the long winter of my life.

Without Jack around, I wouldn't be here.

Life tends to eat away at your soul until there's nothing left. Add heartache and abandonment, and the mountain grows. The past is buried under the dirt, a grave of my own making. The future remains uncertain, but with Jack and Arde, maybe my soul isn't as damned as I once thought.

So, this night is the first of firsts. We splash and swim around while escaping into another round or two until the morning sun greets us both. How we didn't freeze is mind-blowing to me. I suppose with the heat of one another, it's enough.

The sun is symbolic as I walk her home and make my way back to my own.

The night doesn't have to be a terrible thing I run from as long as I remember to let in the light.

That's what they are. Ardella and Jack are the light to my dark, and fuck, it is freeing.

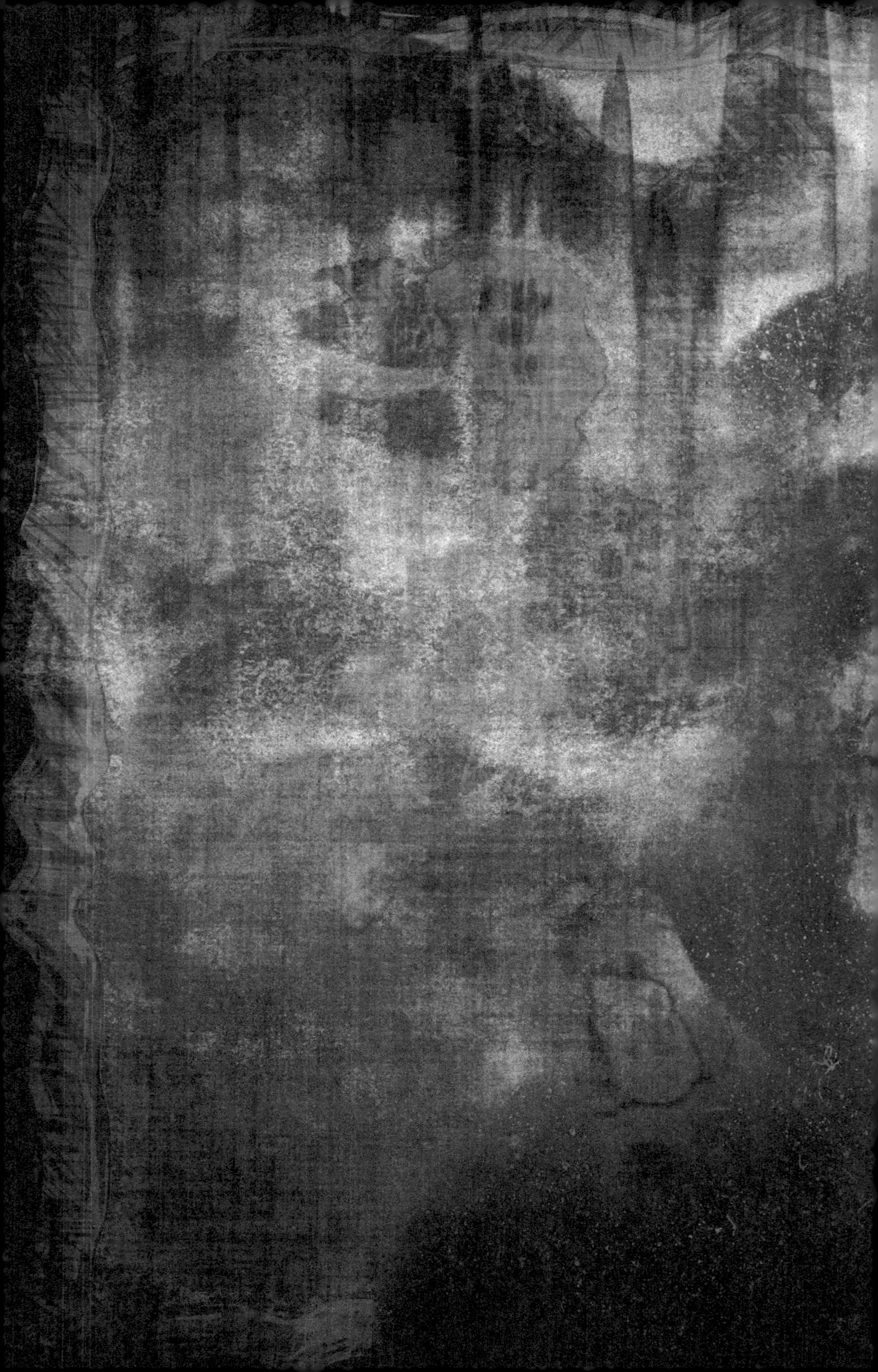

MY SERENADE

Madness has plagued me
A lover's kiss
A quiet cry in the night
For an exposed lover is a beautiful sight

Light and dark become a spectrum of color
A lover's kiss
Shaking under a touch
One more look and it will be too much

A fire burns in the dark Deep and down we go
Endless, swirling, Unfurling

There is no end in sight
My love, deep and dark as perpetual night
Do you feel it?
Whispering, calling

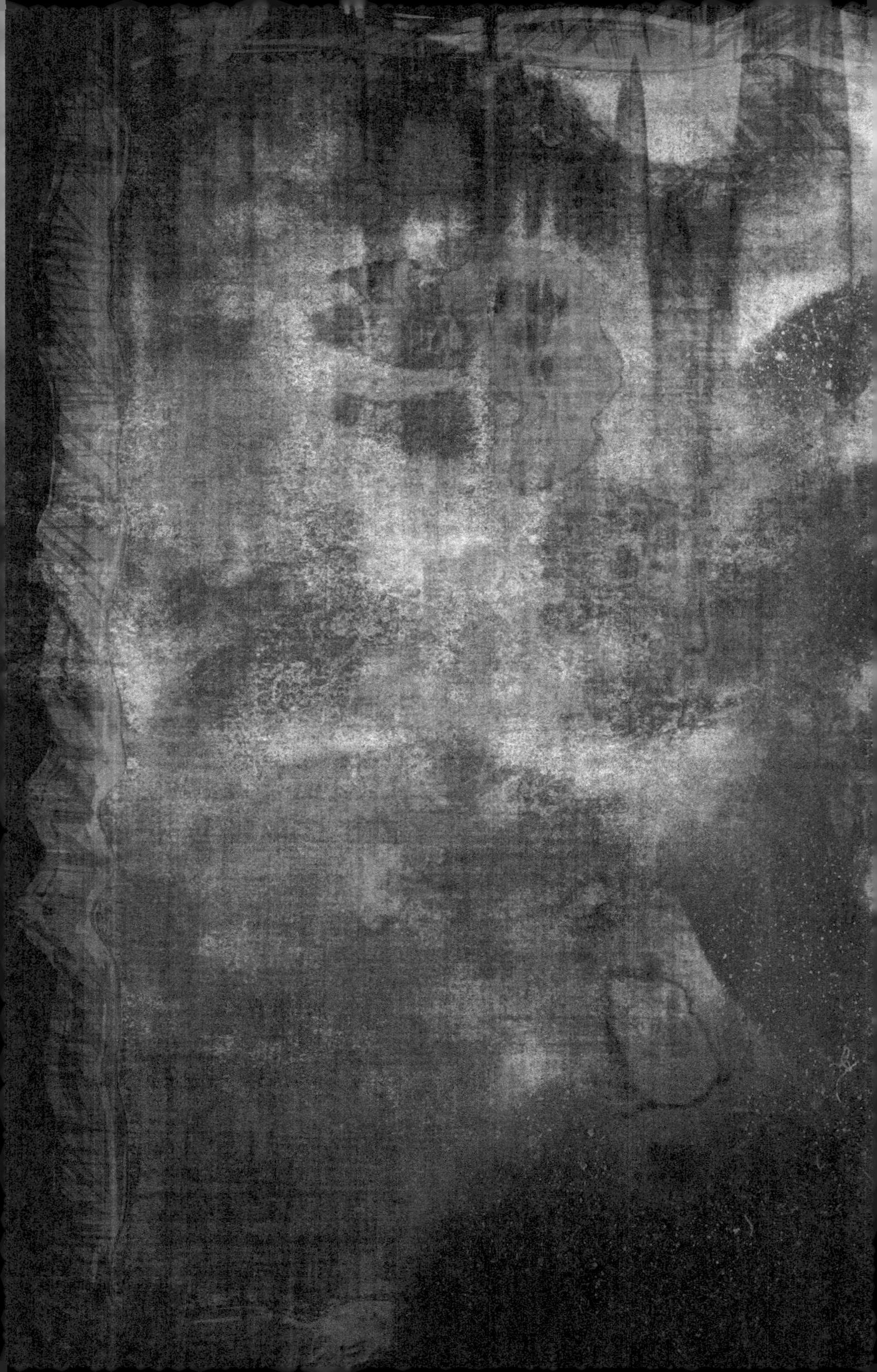

Death's angel is at your door
    Claimed and possessed
    A lover's kiss
    Close thine eyes and it is all bliss

Chained only to you
    A prisoner of your heart
    It burns me,
    Set aflame our old oak tree.

The years pass
    Do you still remember?
    Our lover's kiss
    One you surely miss

Have you forgotten?
    Our hidden secrets,
    Yet death burns in our flames
    Of all that was and will never be
    Our lover's kiss

— E.G. Poa

E.G.POA

CHAPTER TWELVE

ARDELLAN E.G. POA

ARDELLA

Paper after paper flies over my shoulder as I frantically scribble the words. They don't fly out of my head fast enough. Nothing is right. Nothing will do.

Doubt seeps in like poison, straight into my creativity. Gildus *fucking* Furrows.

He's the poison, and apparently, my anonymity is a growing concern amidst the writing community.

It doesn't matter if it's death or love; he finds a way to slander. Only *his* way is right. My blood is boiling from such frustrations.

Gildus is a pompous swine, egotistical and entitled like any other man. The tension rises over my shoulders as I turn to view the mess behind me. Papers and journals are thrown everywhere, scattering all around me; my bed isn't made, and I couldn't remember the last time I showered with the bun upon my head.

Rubbing my eyes, I turn toward the open letter from the Boss Man on the desk.

An invitation to a masquerade to unveil the enemy writers.

The world yearns to know.

What a fucking cliché.

Yet, I need to know who this Prick Furrows is—just like everyone else. He already spells it out for me professionally. I could only imagine the bastard of a man. Old, grumpy, and entitled, no doubt.

Leaning and rubbing my temples with a heavy sigh, the party mentions being held in the city two months from now. I can bring anyone.

I will need a disguise, a clever one. Could I trust Jack and Roman with my secret identity and cause a ruckus with me? Part of me knows the answer, but the other part holds fear.

The only person who knows my identity is Anabel Lee.

Rigswold knew I wrote poetry and stories, but he was out of the picture. Engaged and probably married by now, with children on the way.

A startling ache settles inside my beating chest while I write to my best friend about Gildus threatening to unmask me. *Prick.*

Nothing will be easy for Gildus, and when I see him, I'll slip some poison to him for emotional distress and slander.

To be determined.

I'm not the only one in the house looking unwell; my father and Kenzie are as well.

PAST

She came home out of sorts one weekend, and I braved her grumpiness to try to talk to her.

"Mackenzie, what's wrong?"

I entered her bedroom as she collapsed into her bed as if all life had left her pale blue eyes. She had pale hair like me, but her eyes weren't abnormal like mine.

"Go away, Ardella; what do you care? Don't you have some bodies to prepare or something?"

I exhaled heavily, kneeling beside where she lay sideways on her bed.

"I know I'm not the greatest companion or sister, but I am here now," I offered earnestly.

She merely stared at me with the blankest expression. Like no life was left in her eyes.

What on earth is going on?

"I'm tired, and I do not have the energy right now. Please leave."

My eyes fell as I reached to stroke her hair, and she rolled away, turning her back to me to signify the conversation was over.

"I don't know what's going on, and you don't have to talk to me, but talk to someone. You aren't alone, Kenz. My door is always open for you."

I made my way slowly to her door, turning slightly to catch a glimpse. Her sunken cheeks, and hollow eyes, so petite and frail, lonely even. Broken over something, I then realized. A relationship or feud, maybe?

"You haven't used that name since we were kids..." Her voice sounded small as I recalled all too well.

We played in the dirt and pretended to be explorers on great adventures in our youth. Those adventures ended as we grew, and when I became more fascinated with death than living flesh and dolls. I didn't think she forgave me for it, and perhaps I was the worst sibling when she gravitated toward our mother more. But recalling the past didn't help either of us.

"I know, and I'm sorry for that. I am a fool. I abandoned you for my own obsessions, and I will regret it for the rest of my days. You didn't deserve that from me. There was a weird rift after I began to help Father out in the basement, and Mother couldn't stand it... I'm sorry," I repeated the words silently, the deep melancholic buzz droning my head.

"Everything will be okay someday, Kenz. Maybe not today, but it will get better someday. It has to."

I lingered in her doorway, and when she said nothing else, I left. It was probably the first honest conversation in years. I had hurt her, and there was no easy way to even begin to repair it, so I started with a proper apology. She was old enough to make her own decisions on what she wanted to do with life and whether she wanted to mend things. I couldn't force my sister to love or forgive me. We grew up, and apart—things like that happened.

The least I can do is express my apologies and say that I'm here now if she needs me.

Walking into the kitchen, I grabbed water, my eyes roving over the door to the basement. Gazing at it with contempt for the longest while, I sat at the dining room table, staring into space. As if the universe knew I needed more peculiarities, my father walked inside, kissing the top of my head.

"Why are you staring into space with such a look on your face? As if the world has no hope left?"

I shrugged, not answering him.

"Whatever it is, it will work itself out. It always does in the end."

He grabbed the leftovers and heated them up before sitting next to me.

"We have a service this weekend. Are you available?"

I nodded. It's not the dead's fault. They were dead, after all, no matter how they got there.

"Good, good. I think we need to find more opportunities or think of selling this place." He paused briefly, sighing deeply. "I'm tired, Ella. Money isn't coming in, and I can't keep letting Reyn take everything over. He has his own problems and relationship issues... My gambling got out of control again... I'm supposed to provide for this family, and I'm failing miserably."

I looked up finally. "That's not true. You're doing your best. It's a slow month, we'll figure it out. I can give you the money I make from—"

"*No.*" He spoke so sternly that I blinked in disbelief.

"I'm not taking money from my *daughter*. My son is bad enough, but he pays the bills before I have a chance to say anything."

I reached for his hand, trying to offer some comfort. "What can I do? Please, tell me."

He patted my hand, shaking his head.

"Nothing, lovely girl. I need you to live your life. Kenzie is with whatever drugs and friends she's gotten into, and I need you to live life how you see fit. Can you do that for me, Ella? That would make me happiest to see."

My eyes watered. "Of course, Dad... I just don't want to see you struggle."

Relationship problems? Drugs? Gambling? What the fuck was happening with my family?

"You won't have to; I'll figure something out. You know I love you, right?"

I offered him a worried smile while he leaned, kissing my forehead.

"Now, no more tears or long faces. Eat with me?" He nudged the dish over and handed me a fork.

My heart increased with pressure as I indulged his request, attempting to fake joy just to see him smile and laugh again. He had let me in on a moment of weakness. He regretted it soon after, redirecting the conversation, not wanting to say anything further.

Something was brewing in the air. A misery that lingered in the house. Where I once found joy had become nothing but bitter memories. Like my mother, we were just ghosts in the house of the dead with our vices.

When we finally left the table, I went to my room, finding my sister's dark as I passed it.

Plopping onto my bed, a sense of foreboding came over me. A similar one like when Rigs left all those years ago. The fucked up part, I couldn't do a damn thing about it. Not when everything was broken beyond repair, beginning before my mother's passing. It was only a matter of time before all the seams split.

PRESENT

Jack and Roman aren't around for a couple of weeks as they finally bought their new place. I continue writing erratically. After helping my father with the weekend services, my father and sister disappeared. It is not unusual for Kenzie, but I begin to worry when I don't see my father or hear him around.

I worry about the whole family, but I'm not a part of my siblings' lives; I can't find or control how they live. I don't even know where to start repairing it, either.

The gloomy mood drifts into my writing as I write something dark when a loud knock at the front door interrupts my thoughts. I shut my bedroom door behind me, wondering who it could be. The house is so quiet I wonder where all the ghosts have gone.

It's only me there.

"There she is," Roman croons as I open the door; Jack follows behind with a cute smile.

"I wasn't expecting anyone," I mumble awkwardly, looking down at the white night dress I'm still wearing.

"You look great; nothing either of us hasn't seen," Roman winks, and I huff out a breath.

"Are you hungry or thirsty?" I offer, leading them to the kitchen.

"Never for food." His voice lowers behind me.

"To what do I owe the visit then?" I ask over my shoulder, getting a glass of water for myself.

Something must be wrong with me that I'm not joyful to see them; must be too much on my mind.

"I'm hurt you aren't happy to see me," Roman pouts, appearing at my side as I turn to poke his stomach.

"I'm busy today, much is on my mind," I tell him while downing my water quickly and moving away.

I caught them exchanging glances in my periphery. "Well, that won't do... Jacky?"

I briefly turn to catch Jack closing in on me before throwing me over his shoulder.

"What's your deal?" I wiggle my legs and reach down to smack his ass.

His laugh echoes through the hallway up the stairs. Roman is behind me, looking pleased with himself.

We arrive at my room, and Jack finally sets me down.

Before I can complain, his lips are on mine, stopping me in my tracks.

"Who is E.G. Poa?" I hear Roman ask.

Shit.

I give myself away by freezing up as Jack pulls back, turning to look at Roman by my writing desk.

"It's no one," I try to speak calmly.

Snatching away whatever Roman is reading, I block the desk. He scrunches his brows together, appearing more conflicted, while Jack frowns.

"What are you hiding? Is another man writing you love poetry and notes?" Roman sounds *offended.*

I don't expect it to affect me the way it was, but I swallow it down.

When I don't answer fast enough, Roman continues. "Are we not enough for you?"

"No, that's not—"

"Come on, Jack, we were wrong about her," he says, and they hang their heads and begin to walk toward the door.

The hurt in his tone and them walking away from me causes a knot to twist in my chest that I'm not equipped to handle.

"Wait!"

When they don't stop, I take a significant risk. "It's not a man, it's *me.*"

The confession halts them in their tracks. "Please, sit. I'll explain..."

I fiddle with my fingers nervously as they both sit at the edge of the bed, watching me with curiosity and skepticism.

"Will you protect my secrets?" I ask them first and foremost.

They're staring at me, and all I can think of is how wonderful it will be to have them both filling me while we tangle in the sheets. The image pops into my mind, seeing them sitting there on my bed, waiting for me to finish my confession.

"That all depends on you, and if there's no man involved..." Roman's voice is possessive, sending a chill through my bones.

"There's no man, for Christ's sake."

"I don't know if you realized this or not, but you are *our* girl.

We don't share."

I raise my eyebrow in question as Jack nods in agreement with Roman's proclamation. "So, I'm a possession to you both then?"

My earlier crankiness changes into whatever is unfolding in my room. *I really need to get a grip on my life.*

Their eyes darken, showing their answer as heat floods. I can picture it in full with their hands both roaming to claim every inch of skin, making and taking what's theirs.

I'm theirs, and they're *mine.*

"Yes. We possess that delicious body of yours, make no mistake," Roman adds.

I close my eyes briefly, breathing out slowly to gather my thoughts. "I didn't realize all three of us are...together."

Jack leans forward. "I hope it's clear now."

Gripping the edge of the desk, I rub my thighs together, wetting my lips.

No, don't get distracted. Finish what you started.

"There's no one else... I write under an alias. People don't take women writers seriously, so I use my middle names instead of my first. I write for a paper column...stories, poetry, and sometimes critiques."

I hand them a few pages of completed works as a peace offering.

They lean in unison and take a look at them.

"What does the E and G stand for?" Jack wonders aloud, glancing up briefly as I move to sit in the chair in front of the bed.

"Esther Gray... Ardellan E.G. Poa. I don't like or use my full name, so Ardella is the name I use for people that matter. I use my other initials for professionalism. I've never had to meet anyone for my job; it's mailed in, and it's how I'm paid."

"Beautiful, even still," Jackson says sweetly with a boyish smile that I adore and melt over it.

"However," I warn, "if I ever hear my full name, I will be done with you both. Is that understood? You're lucky I let you get away with Arde."

Roman grins wickedly, spelling out the upcoming trouble. "You write dark and lovely things, *Ardellan.*" I jump up and tackle him into bed.

"What did I tell you!" I poke him roughly on his sides and stomach.

Jack takes the paper from his hands, reading it while I torture Roman.

The man himself is giggling like a child, so much that I blush and find it all hysterical. It's priceless to find him ticklish and acting boyish. My heart dissolves even more when he captures my lips, stopping and easing my mind altogether.

It's my turn to get it, and he starts tickling me.

I try to pull away, and we burst into laughter, and for a moment, I forget *'my tales of woe.'*

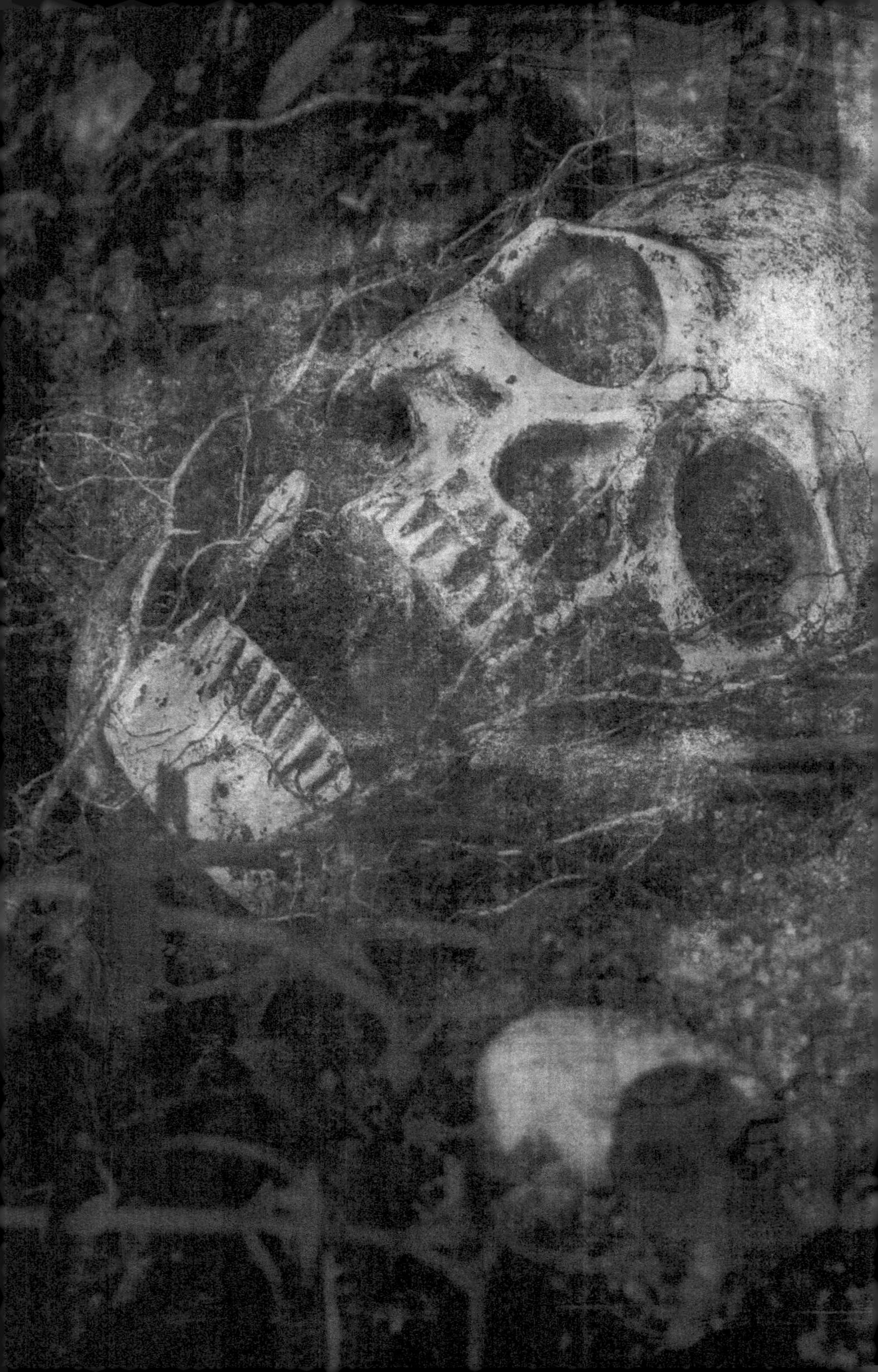

HIDE AND SEEK

Mortal, but immortal amongst these pages
  To live on forevermore
  A gift of creative means,
  Told and torn through the ages

Are you friend or foe?
  Dream or seem? Life or death?
  My salvation or my undoing

Can you catch me amongst the trees?
  Was that a shadow or was it me?
  Lurking
  Toying

You hide, and I seek
  Only I write the words to their peak
  The big unveiling
  Who is it that you seek?

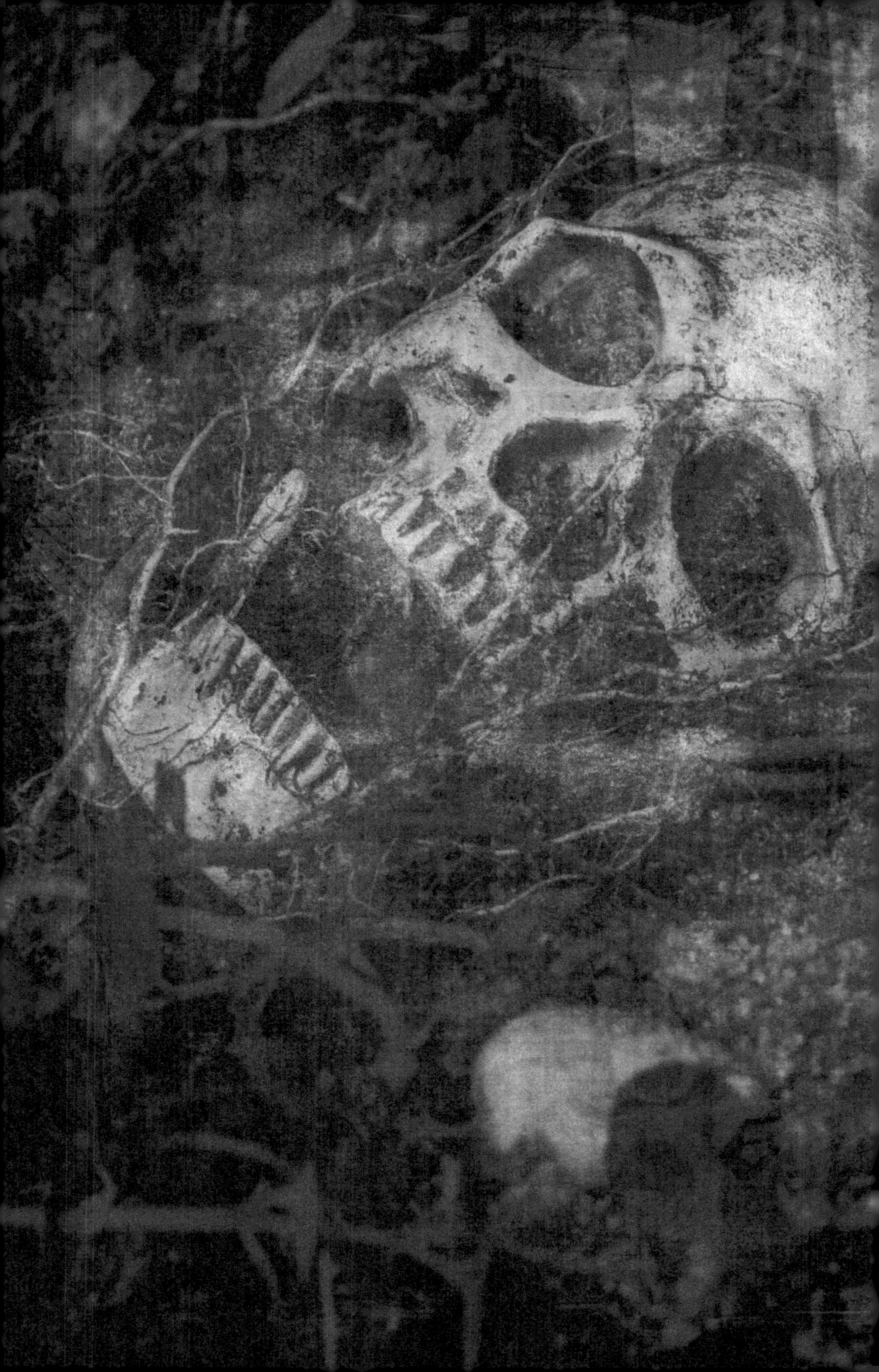

Man or woman? Dog or cat?
    Monster or a witch at that
    Questions, so many questions

A poet's heart,
    Is theirs to reveal
    Their face, their name
    Is their own

No one can take that away
    So, play this game
    Unwind and untamed Will you find me?

Amidst your friends,
    Or past lovers
    A teacher by all rights
    Words amidst the masked will not be my undoing
tonight

At my discretion, only then will I appear
    Or I will disappear
    You will not come near
    For it is me you should fear

— E.G. Poa

CHAPTER THIRTEEN

MY LADY OF DEATH

JACK

The time has finally come. Ardella is mine. *Ours,* rather.

Leave it to Roman to claim her entirely, but at least I got my first taste.

Today is the day to claim her solo. I set up a date beforehand for something more suitable for Ardella's dark mind.

When I pick her up from her house, she's wearing a flowy white dress, pale like a ghost. I lead her on a long walk to consecrated grounds.

Only the best for My Lady Of Death.

"A cemetery date? You shouldn't have," she coos, and I squeeze her hand.

The air has warmed slightly, even with the sun hiding behind the clouds. Ideal for such a day.

"Yes, but not quite," I mention quietly, leading her to the underground mausoleum.

My family's mausoleum.

It's relatively old, covered in vines, and surrounded by trees at the cemetery's edge. There are multiple in the cemetery, but the one I lead her to is large enough to wander into.

All of my family lie within that tomb, fallen to misfortune and disease, leaving me a boy without a home all those years ago until Roman gave that to me.

Ardella's eyes light up while I open the door, and down the stairs we go. The place is less dusty since I swept beforehand. I can smell the vanilla in the air, wafting through the stone hallway lined with gothic sconces that open to the larger room.

"You know, as much as I love and respect where the dead rest, I've never physically gone into a mausoleum. I'm impressed that you broke in, bringing—"

She freezes, taking inventory of the candle display with the red roses scattered all around her. There are no open tombs since it has been decades since any of my relatives had been buried.

There before us, lining the wall, is a large gray centralized block at the center of the back wall. It's that tomb that's easily seen from the hallway upon entry. It's my great-grandfather's.

"I'm impressed, Jack. Who knew you were a romantic?" Her eyes reflect the flames, sending an electric jolt straight through me.

"I wanted to fuck you somewhere creatively for the first time. More suitable to your *tastes*. Is it too much?"

A smile lifts from those delectable lips. "No. You are a man after my own morbid heart."

I reach for her hand and bring her closer to me.

"Where should I worship you first?" I murmur against her lips.

Her delicate hands pull at my light coat. I'm already hot and bothered, so the draft aids in cooling my skin. Once I toss my coat elsewhere, I back her against the large gray block, claiming her lips for a few moments while she unbuttons my long-sleeved white shirt, tossing it once she finishes.

"I know where I'll have you first," I interrupt, kneeling before her and pressing my nose right into her cunt.

Breathing her in, Ardella's hand slips into my hair, combing her fingers as if to encourage me further. My eyes close in complete bliss as her feminine scent fills me. I run a hand under her dress, up her thigh slowly. I use my other hand to caress her outer thigh.

When I realize she's bare, I close my eyes.

"My naughty girl. You knew what I had planned for you, didn't you?"

"I was hoping as much..."

I move my eyes up slowly, meeting her yellow ones. "I'll make it a reality, My Lady of Death."

I rise, lifting her so she can sit at the edge of the surface. My greatgrandfather, a guy I'd never met, is underneath her, but I'm sure he wouldn't mind such an intrusion. Surely, the old man supports such lust.

"You don't think the man underneath the slab will mind, right?" She giggles as if reading my thoughts for herself.

"I think any man would approve of such worship. Better to apologize later and live without regrets." My mouth lifts to one side, lifting her dress so I can gaze at the pussy I'm hungry for.

A complacent look remains on her while spreading her legs so I can kneel before her once more. Admiring her glistening lips, I lightly trail my lips up her thigh before swiftly maneuvering her legs over my shoulders.

"This is mine," I whisper, holding her in place as I lick firmly up her wet slit.

Ardella leans back as I hold her in place, tasting her essence and reveling in such a treasure. The way she swells and how her thighs squeeze my skull... Her reactions are made solely for me, this day, at least. I'll share her with Roman soon enough. Perhaps he and I will taste each other more intimately before then. The thought makes me moan while I flick my tongue and tease her clit in easy strokes. I begin to suck once she twitches.

"Yes," she encourages, enabling me to bring her further into my depths.

Making vibrating sounds against her, she's absolutely sinful, *addicting*. Her scent and how wet she is, it's my siren call of death. Death to my final resting place, right between her thighs, *her soul*. I am lost at sea and drowning in her. *So fucking perfect.*

"I could do this all night," I mention, before sinking two fingers inside.

Her hands scrunch into my hair, gripping and pulling as I bring her to meet her maker.

She cries out my name while I force her to fully ride it out, shaking and nearly suffocating me with the death grip of her thighs. *Fuck me, I can get used to this.*

I suck harder on her clit, curling my fingers while she dives into the sea of deathly bliss with me. Her inner walls are hugging my fingers, coming on my face so beautifully that I never want to leave.

Her eyes finally fly to my own as she relaxes backward, along with her grip on my hair. Her breathing is uneven, and I rejoice, grunting in approval. I nibble on her thigh before adjusting her legs, standing between them to gaze down at her with eyes half-lidded.

"Look at you, so satiated, My Morbid Angel. Receiving pleasure in a mausoleum does it for you, hmm?"

I nestle myself between her legs while she wraps her legs around me, sitting up quickly and tugging at my pants desperately.

"Fuck yes, it does." She's panting for me as I fully kick off the rest of what I'm wearing.

"What would you like next?" I ask, teasing her cunt with my tip.

I'm so hard it hurts.

She does it for me.

Pushing herself so my tip glides inside, we stifle our gasps in unison, eyes locking on each other until I'm in fully. My eyes drift close, transfixing on how fucking good and warm she is. The space between us is finally being filled, bringing us closer than ever before.

She is my sanctuary amongst the dead, breathing more life into me.

The sound of her voice makes my eyes open slowly as she speaks suddenly, "I want you to fuck me. Then, I want you to bend me over and fuck me *harder*."

Her honest response makes me smile as I circle my arms around her, pulling her closer to claim her swollen lips that are begging to be kissed. She's already so wet for me. The stretch of her is welcoming while she clutches to me, nails digging into my back.

"Finally, my dreams are coming true," I tell her, before slamming back inside.

Her mouth falls open, moaning before taking my face between her hands. With those bright, burning yellow eyes remaining on me, I nearly lose it with such intense eye contact.

"You're better than I imagined. Although, I have no complaints with that devilish tongue of yours," she mentions as more sweet sounds leave her.

Claiming her mouth, I swirl my tongue with hers, knowing she can taste herself.

Her body molds perfectly to mine. Minus her dress that's still in my way. I pause my thrusts briefly to help her out of it before placing her ankles at my shoulders so I can hit deeper and see those glorious tits bounce for me.

Those cries turn into screams, my name a prayer on her lips, but also a plea for more. Her inner walls begin to tighten around me as I ease, helping her up before turning her around to fuck her harder as she requests of me.

Ardella grips the edge, bent over and ready as I slide back home.

Not wanting to disappoint her, I begin slowly before quickly shifting to a fast, hard pace. Reaching my hand forward, I wrap her hair around my hand, tugging slightly as her cries reverberate through stone walls. A symphony in this tomb. Enough to raise the dead.

The lighting of the candles around us paints her as an artistic display before me: sin and pleasure, yet beauty and madness. Love is churning within me. Love for this precious woman.

At the realization, I hold her tight, moving my hand from her hair to her throat, lightly holding it before squeezing. Nudging her flush against the edge, I ram her ruthlessly. Those strangled cries are heaven to my ears. She soon tightens around my cock, falling over the edge, bringing me with her.

"I'm going to fuck you until you can't walk, and just when you think I'm done, I'm going to do it again..."

"Please," she begs.

I stiffen, filling her up with all of me as her pussy hugs me tight, pulsing with me, falling into the abyss of pleasure. In heaving breaths, I lean my head against her back, releasing my hold on her throat. I don't add too much pressure as I'm not sure if she's into breath play or choking, so I go for the middle ground of the illusion with a light squeeze. As I lead her down towards the blanket on the floor, a long exhale leaves us both.

Helping her out of her shoes, I move them to the side

before leaning down to kiss up her body, meeting her lips. I do it for a while before I have her on all fours, screaming, until no surface in that room goes untouched, minus the ceiling since it was out of reach. *I'm sure we'd fuck up there if we could.*

Ardella is everything I need and more. I can't wait until Ro and I have her together. Fuck, I can't wait to taste them *both* on my tongue. My heart is big enough for two. That will come in all due time. Hopefully, Roman is on the same page.

He is already with Ardella, but I'm not sure about *me.*

I got my first fill of Ardella on our mausoleum date. Just when her eyes are half-lidded, ready to close, I sneak in another round with her in my lap. Her cries bounce off the walls, and she orgasms while our eyes roll into the back of our skulls; *all of it is my deadly sanctuary.* Ardella has a complete hold over me, and I'm already finding I can't get enough.

I make sure we're both overly spent and panting by the time we leave the mausoleum at dawn.

We blow out the candles before leaving. I'll clean it all up after I take her home.

Her hand never leaves mine as we make our way, ending up at her doorstep, kissing. I can see her exhaustion, how she appears ready to pass out at any minute.

"I'm delightfully sore. I'll be dreaming of you," she says dreamily, swaying into me.

I release a low chuckle, kissing her head before she walks in. "Get some rest, My Lady of Death. I'll see you soon. I will most certainly be dreaming about you."

With one last smile, she leaves me there, and I quickly make my way to clean everything up because I also feel the edges of sleep beckoning me.

All that is left to do is figure out where Roman stands with everything regarding me and him...

When I finally arrive home, I find Roman asleep on the

couch. He's on his back with his arm above his head, wearing lounge pants and a shirt. A simple but alluring look on him.

I have admired everything about him for as long as I can remember. Growing up, he was there with me, my best friend —*my everything*. I wouldn't have made it through life without him. *We* survived.

Smiling fondly at the little boy who grew into a handsome man, I lay a blanket gently over him before heading to my room to try and sleep. It takes me a while to finally sleep, for two people I love most haunt my wakeful dreams.

ROMANCE

One look, your touch
    My heart you took, it's full of so much
    There's a story book within that touch

Flesh and bone
    You unfold and devour
    I'll never know again what it means to be alone
    Within my darkest hour

There you are
    Brightly lit, my perfect star
    I did not think I'd go so far
    You and me, so bizarre

The novelty and strangeness,
    Of what it means to love
    And be loved
    Unseen by many

What we know to be true
    Is that I belong to you
    Running through the meadows
    No longer alone with our shadows

Life to my spirit,
    Singing your song
    Love me now, we'll never go wrong
    My heart is yours alone

When our lives pass us by,
    We await our end
    For you alone, I will cry
    Into the pile of death, we'll descend

You and me
    Forever we will be
    Along with this memory
    You and me

—E.G. Poa

E.G. POA

CHAPTER FOURTEEN

MACKENZIE

ARDELLA

"My Requiem."

I tap my pencil against my cheek. The words will not write themselves. All I had was the damn *title.* That's the problem with writing, conjuring the words to truly express whatever the message; there are a *million* different ways to do so.

What do I want my requiem to say? Should it be thought provoking, or darkly romantic? Perhaps morbid, like always?

I toss the paper, lightly banging my head on my desk. There is much frustration over the words that fail to write themselves. I debate whether I want to lie amongst the dead for inspiration or bother my lovers. *Something's got to give.*

Before I can decide, a hard knock echoes through the house.

Sitting up slowly in confusion, I do a mental tally. Neither of my family members have been home for weeks, and there's no service. It's odd, considering people die *all the time.*

All I can do is write and write.

With trepidation, I make my way downstairs, hesitant to open the door. The knock didn't sound like Roman or Jackson, so it could be anyone.

Knock, knock!

Opening it slowly, *cautiously,* two men in black uniforms stand before me. The more I look, the more I realize they're police officers local to Morella.

They take off their hats. Oh, that's *not* good. My heart races in anticipation like jolts of lightning through a stormy sky.

"Is there anyone else in the home with you, ma'am?"

I shake my head. "I'm Jonathan Poa's daughter. This is our home and place of business."

The gentlemen nod politely while a slight tremor spreads to my fingers.

"Would you like to come in?" I offer, letting them inside as they thank me.

Something is wrong. But *what?*

Leading them into the sitting area, my palms begin to sweat, and my mind races at such a realization. Everyone knows when the hats come off, *death* is involved. *But who?*

My father?

"We bring troublesome news..." The one on the right speaks, fidgeting with his hat, "Mackenzie Poa was found in the river outside the city; no foul play was involved. It was deemed intentional... It's outside our jurisdiction... so we wanted to know how to proceed. We tried to contact your father and a male named Reynolds."

"That's my brother," I say without fully processing.

Mackenzie.

"Yes," the other cop chimes in. "We haven't been able to contact either. Reynolds has been unreachable in the city, and no one at his firm office has seen him. Apparently, he rushed out suddenly over a week ago, but nothing since. His fiancé hasn't heard a word either."

Reyn has a fiancé... *Interesting.*

"Have her brought here. I will make the arrangements," I say on principle, the thoughts not quite registering.

"Do you need any assistance? There's another funeral service across town that may be willing to help."

I look at both men, nodding. I can't *lift* a casket by myself.

"We will send word within a couple of days, Miss Poa."

"Thank you. Hopefully, my brother and father can be reached soon. This is unusual of them since this is their business," I tell them as they stand respectfully.

Part of me wonders if they are expecting me to start sobbing.

I can't admit a woman is running the show, not when I need the help.

"Please let us know if you need anything at all."

"Of course. Thank you, gentlemen. Let me know if you find or hear word of my brother or my father," I say as they leave and wave them politely off.

I watch through the window as they pull away from the large gravel driveway. I look at the black hearse parked off to the side and sigh heavily.

Their words echo in my mind on a loop. Looking around at the walls in the too quiet house, it suddenly feels too imposing. The silence roams heavily until all I can hear is my own heartbeat.

Thump, thump.

Had I taken the news non-empathetically?

It has to be shock. That's the only reason I can think of... Looking down, my hands shake.

Oh.

Refusing to stay in the empty house to process, I snatch my

coat and throw on my boots, disappearing into the woods. I travel toward the backside of the house, avoiding any glances toward the graveyard attached or the seemingly looming crematorium.

Too dark, I can't think of that now.

I can't say how long I wander, but darkness washes over me.

My mind is numb, and I cannot be certain of how to feel. I'm a stranger in my sister's life. She must've gotten mixed up with something more than drugs, as unresponsive and withdrawn as she was. I didn't realize she was struggling in that way or...wanting to end her life. I can only do what I can do. Perhaps me apologizing happened too late.

I should've done more.

The trickling water pulls me from the haze of my mind when I spot my favorite bathing place.

The water is ordinarily bearable for me, but when I step in, it is chilly. It's as if Mother Nature knows I need to feel something. *Anything.*

I lay all my clothes carefully out as I hiss at the temperature as I wade in.

Once I'm fully underwater, I open my eyes in the dark and wonder what my sister's last thoughts were. Did she slip? Jump? Was it impulsive? Maybe the city cops have it wrong, and she was mixed up with bad people and was murdered?

Somehow, in my heart, I know the dreadful answer. Our family is cursed with death.

I open my mouth into the darkness, releasing a scream until my lungs are empty. The water drowns the sounds until I come up for air.

There is no moon to light my way home.

Endless dark and endless night. Death and decay, just like

I'd be someday. Down, I am slipping into the void, processing the present and what to do next.

I am the only woman left. My father and brother are officially missing.

Were each of us cursed to misery?

Sinking back under, where I am in my own little empty, dark space. That's when I break.

When my lungs become tight, I rise out of the water, finally letting my tears fall. Quiet sobs and floating on my back, I let myself feel it. The unshakable grief. The past mistakes or overlooks.

Kenzie deserved so much more than my tears. I should have been there for her instead of living in my own little world. Instead of tending to the dead and focusing more on being a child but no, I abandoned her, just as our mother did. Because death seeps deep within our morbid family.

I need to find my father and wherever the hell Reyn disappeared to.

But first, I need to bury my sister.

I have to be the one to prepare her and give her a beautiful day. It's always ill-advised for family members in the business, but I don't give a damn. I couldn't be there for her in the way she needed, but I'd make up for it in death.

Two days later, I'm doing my sister's makeup. Ensuring she looks her best, my heart is still in a stalemate.

Lost in my thoughts, I see how peaceful she looks dead. How great she looks in pale blue, the color she always wore when we were kids. It's how I want to remember her. From a better time when I was a better sister.

There is no scowl or unhappiness. Most people look that way to me, though, so maybe it was biased.

Time is fleeting, unwinding, but never stopping. Where was she now? Did she ever find a religion or belief? Was she stuck somewhere that was just as grueling, a purgatory perhaps?

Despite these thoughts, somehow, I feel as if wherever she is, it's more peaceful than our death ridden life.

Upon finishing, I let the two men from another funeral home assist with her casket preparation. I set her up with her limbs being propped up while I ensure the viewing room is decorated with gorgeous bright flowers that I knew she had always loved.

I can recall her pale eyes lighting up with joy when we were younger and flower picking. I stuck to my cool-toned palettes while she chose bright colors. I wonder what happened to her light. Was it our mother? Was it me? Our family? A rebellious life we didn't know about?

A breath leaves me as I take note of my finishing touches. It smells lovely in the viewing room, so floral and *alive*, at least how most fresh flowers are initially.

Roman and Jackson show up, and they are probably the only ones I know that do. Not many people stop in, and my heart dies a little more. My sister was as isolated as I am...

Would anyone show up to my funeral?

"Don't say anything or ask how I'm doing. Just help me get through this day." I probably sound pitiful when I tell them, but they do not judge as they linger nearby at all times, until it's time to close up shop.

I let them hug me and kiss either side of my cheeks when they originally arrived earlier. My hug was a half assed attempt, too, but I appreciated them showing up for me and a sister they didn't know. I stayed in her room every night before then, smelling her floral scent, reminding me of innocence and secrets. Secrets of her life I'd never know.

Once I lock up for the night after the service, I curl up into my bed, utterly numb with both men on either side of me.

I appreciate that for one day and night, Roman is quiet. No bickering or banter. He probably knew I wasn't ready for it. Jack was better at reading the room, albeit an empty one, but gracious about it, nonetheless.

The morning after, the small funeral in the family graveyard is equally uneventful. I say nothing but goodbye, laying a pale blue rose on her casket. A few local officials show up out of respect.

Still no Reyn or Dad.

When it's just the three of us, standing at her grave alone, I mutter bitterly, "I made sure not to put anything valuable in her casket."

I catch them looking at each other as I walk away, ready to melt into the earth, too.

There's no denying that I'd be grieving my father or brother next. I can't tell one morbid thought from the next.

"Do you want to go to the diner or see a different view for a while?" Roman asks solemnly as a driver takes us away from my house.

"I don't care," I say in a weird, monotone way that's unlike me, while staring outside the window at the day's gloom.

We end up at the diner. Food isn't appealing, but a chocolate milkshake certainly does the trick.

"It's good to see you're eating something," Roman states as their food is brought out, along with my milkshake.

I say nothing in response as Jack moves to sit beside me, lightly rubbing my knee to let me know that I am not alone. I appreciate his gesture before he moves his hand to his plate to dig in. Roman's eyes watch me from across the table as I close mine and enjoy the rich taste of milk chocolate.

"Do you want to come with us to see our new place? It's a simple house near the library." Jack is the one who breaks the silence, and I shrug instead of responding.

"Please tell us if there's anything we can do and how we can best help you..."

I look up at Roman. "I'm enjoying the peace and quiet. You normally talk too much."

My gaze moves back to the milkshake in front of me as his foot rubs mine under the table.

"That's better," is all he says.

I suppose he needed to know I was still on planet Earth, not sinking entirely into the dark. Not *yet,* anyway. I'm always in the dark, though.

As they finish eating, I decide to ask, "Do you have your own rooms?"

Roman answers, his tone becoming lighter, "Well, when you spend most of your life sharing one, I thought it was only fair to give Jacky Boy here his own room to brood in."

The man himself scoffs as amusement dances in Roman's brown eyes.

I lean against Jack. "I'll brood with you."

"Thank you, love," he tells me before giving Roman a raised brow look. His smile still remains as I gaze at him across the table.

"When I'm not drowning in grief, I need you both to tell me whether we will be together or not. All of us."

Roman blinks, looking from me to Jack. I angle my head to look at him.

"Is that what you want?" Jack asks me directly, not looking across the table.

I can't tell by his expression whether he's for it or on the fence about it.

"Naturally, but only if you both are comfortable. Can't say I haven't imagined watching you two together..."

Jack blushes, ignoring us both as he sips his water. I have my answer simply watching him react. Putting my head back on his shoulder, I see a dark desire pooling in Roman's eyes, but he says nothing initially while casually observing Jack and me.

"When that day comes, just tell us. I hope you'll participate instead of only watching, though, not that I'd mind either." The look he gives Jack makes my toes curl, but I know I'm not in the right headspace to take action on either scenario.

"Will you both hold me again tonight?"

"Whatever you need, Yellow Eyes." Roman reaches across the table for my hand, and I take it.

"Of course," Jack whispers, kissing my forehead.

It takes us no time at all to pay and leave. I grab both of their hands as they stay on either side of me, leading the way to their new place.

A KNOCK AT THE DOOR

Strange shadows swirl outside in the mist
    Telltale lies in a kiss
    If it is real, I do not know
    Close the shades, my ghosts will no longer show

A knock comes at my door
    Curious, I move my feet swiftly on the floor
    Darkness rising
    Yearning for more, more, more

Throwing it open, no one is there
    I slam the door, too drained to care
    Life is no longer a mystery, too dull
    Fatigued, my eyelids droop at a pull

My dreams are no longer dreams
    My soul's infraction no longer redeemed
    Day into night,
    At my age, I have lost my fight

The end is my calling
In my sleep, I am falling
Down, down, down
Even when I'm gone, the world still goes around

Startled awake,
The frustration I can no longer take
Leery, oh so dreary
With my senses, everything feels eerie

Once more, there is a knock at the door
I look again and it is death,
My eternity forevermore
Electricity igniting my skin,
Cleansed of all my sins

Down I drop into Death's sweet embrace
Lovely peace, so close I can taste
Gazing upon her face, it is so sweet
Past wrongs gone; wouldn't it be so neat?

A gentle kiss,
So close that I do not miss
Life and its fragilities,
How the darkness claims me
No more will I ever be

—E.G. Poa

E.G. POA

ARDELLA

The three of us are sitting at one of the back tables in the library, reading. The stacks of books and hard shelves encase us in our own private solitude.

When we initially entered, I cracked a joke at Roman when he grabbed a book off another shelf.

"You know how to read?" I asked in mock surprise.

His eyes narrowed while Jack snickered, and I bit my cheeks to contain my laugh.

Before I could walk past, he reached out, pulling me to him and poking my side.

"I'll show you later how well I can read, Arde."

I shivered while he nipped at my earlobe, and I squirmed at the sound of his future promise of revenge.

Kissing me swiftly, that wicked grin lingered in my mind as I searched for something to read.

Sitting at the table, my toes curl at the thought of Roman's earlier warning of punishment to my flesh and how pleasurable it would be. *Damn.*

Shifting in my seat, the man himself looks up from whatever he's reading, quirking a brow.

"So, tell us about this enemy writer?" Roman asks randomly, distracting my thoughts away from sex.

The masquerade reveal is now two weeks away.

"He's an asshole. Presumed to be a male just like they probably assume with me."

Both men consider each other, speaking with their secret thoughts I'm not a part of.

"Do you want us to go with you?" Jack questions quietly.

I glance briefly at Roman. "As if you'd give me a choice in the matter."

With a grin, he practically purrs, *"Good girl."*

I roll my eyes and try to ignore the warmth between my thighs at his words. *How he loved to get under my skin in every way he could.*

Jack nudges him, shaking his head. "As much as we don't want to part from you, it is your choice, unlike *that* prick. We care about you, Ardella, so we want to help support you in any way we can."

I reach for his hand and bring it to my lips for a kiss of thanks.

"I need you both there... Should we plan for something? I can show you all the articles I've hidden away with my nemesis. I expect an old fool who thinks he knows everything about creativity and art."

Handsome smiles bless their faces while I nearly swoon in my seat.

They are MINE.

"Until we know exactly who this person is, we want to protect you... I think Jacky Boy here will have a better time convincing the crowd than me. I do want to go as your official date and run off unwanted suitors." With the curl of his lip, he winks.

I lean back lazily in my chair, amused by his words, while crossing my arms over my chest. "What makes you think I'd have problems with other men or that I'm not capable of shooing them away?"

Roman answers matter-of-factly, "Because no sane man, or insane for that matter, will be able to resist the pull of those yellow eyes. You are deadly walking perfection. So beautiful," his gaze travels up and down in admiration, "that all you would need is just one look to bring a man to his knees."

I warm even more under his stare, his *words*.

"It's certainly our favorite place to be," Jack speaks faintly in agreement.

If they keep it up with their words, my thighs will be soaked.

I'm needy enough for them.

Shifting in my seat, I uncross my arms. My mind is entirely blank. The romance on their lips is already pulling me under, and I'd gladly drown in the sea of them. The imagery of having them at the same time tugs me into lustful thoughts, ones I crave so desperately.

"Should I wear a sack and a different shade of eyes?" I wonder aloud, and Roman shakes his head with a huff.

"No, sunshine, make them sweat while we dance with you as lovers do."

Melting over him, I start to wonder if we are truly lovers. Neither of us has spoken any official words, but it shows in their actions.

"I only had one other lover before when I was younger and more foolish. I had flings in college, of course, but nothing permanent. Other than sexual exploration to my *fun* tastes..."

Their eyes light up as they lean on the table. "My first love had moved away after his parents died. I didn't see him again until college, and he was with another woman—*engaged*."

I swallow the bitterness down. Surely, he's married off by now, and I'm only but an afterthought of his past. Why does it still get to me?

"What was his name?" Jack inquires.

"Rigswold, Rigs for short. We never shared any other names, so, I don't know his last name. The sign on our home wasn't repainted with the lettering until I was away at college, so Rigswold never knew what our mortuary services were called all those years ago."

They consider me, nodding ever so slightly.

"Well, Rigs is an idiot for choosing anyone else. I would've come back for you, Yellow Eyes."

Appreciating Roman's unfurling passion, my eyes mist over.

I can see how the darkness has left his eyes, being replaced by something else, something lighter and sweeter.

"I would've, too," Jack confirms alongside him.

I reach for their hands and kiss their knuckles. "Thank you."

"You are ours to taste. Your body, your spirit—*ours*. Someday, we'll be worthy enough to have your heart."

I stare at Jack after he speaks, deciding to fess up and offer *my* truth.

"You both already do."

There's a pause, a silent understanding, while our eyes lock. "I have a mind to take you over this table for all to see as we take turns giving you a high that only *we* can give."

Goddammit, Roman.

I rise slowly in a challenge, feeling feverishly wet. "That mouth of yours is going to get you into trouble, Ro."

His eyes flash as I lightly tap the table, pointing at it.

"This table, you say?" I ask, hoping that my lowkey seduction is working on them.

Jack's gorgeous eyes turn hungry.

"Yes, *this* very table. *Do you want a demonstration, Ardella?*" Jack counters back in a softening tone that makes my knees weak.

He rises while I sit on the table's edge with my back to Roman. Jack strolls around, appearing before me. I pull up my dress, revealing myself bare to him.

Jack runs his fingers over his jawline in contemplation, groaning at the sight.

"Why don't you show me then?" I toy, reaching and pulling him closer.

He grunts once, leaning to capture my needy lips with his. Swirling his tongue with mine, I move his hand to my pussy where he strokes me languidly three times. Sighing out with bliss and remembrance, I tease him by taking his hand and sucking his fingers at my leisure, tasting myself.

The desire he gives me in a single look makes me quiver. Sinking before me, Jack glances up slightly before bringing that tongue down to where his fingers were previously, drawing out the strokes.

My eyes close briefly, leaning back on my elbows to find Roman's heat-filled stare, hovering and observing how Jack indulges in me. Turned on by the sight of both watching one another, Roman's hand slips down the top of my dress, freeing my breast before taking the peak between his fingers. I muffle a sound, running my hand through Jack's curly red hair.

His moans pulse low against my inner walls while he licks with intent, plunging his tongue inside and toying with my clit. Trying to remain quiet, I bite my lip, breathing heavily through my nose.

Roman's lips graze down my jaw, helping me sit up before moving himself to sit behind me.

"Ride his tongue like a good little raven," he murmurs in my ear.

With the way he's holding and teasing my breast, I become overwhelmed by the sensations of their lips and hands working in tandem. My cunt is throbbing and swelling at their ministrations.

Gripping the table with one hand, my other shoots back to Jack's hair to do the same. He takes my clit into his mouth, sucking and sinking two fingers inside. My hips motion in sync with him as I lean my head back against Roman's shoulder, moaning quietly with my eyes rolling back.

Their touches are electrifying currents, awakening my bloodstream and those little satisfying nerves at the top of my pussy.

I come apart, falling into them. My juices cover Jack, his low growling of approval undoing me more.

"Fuck me, this is this one of the sexiest sights I've ever seen. Goddamn."

Turning my head to the side, I pull Roman's mouth to meet mine, stifling his groan.

I release Jack from my grip, pulling my lips away from Roman to narrow my eyes playfully.

"Your turn, darling," I say, and he stays silent, watching me for a moment before both men switch places.

As they do, they share the briefest of glances. Instead of Jack behind me, like Roman was previously, he assists by helping me up, taking my place to sit, and simply holding me in his lap.

Roman kneeling before me is a wondrous sight in itself. *Especially when it shuts him up.*

Leaning into Jack, he trails kisses down my neck. His

cock is rigid against me, and I ground against him. Sighing lightly in my ear, his hand cups my breast. My legs part once more, and it isn't long before my thighs are tight against Roman's head while his tongue descends upon me with such vigor.

"Fuck," is all I can say to his assaulting mouth.

Jack treats my pussy like a lover, and Roman simply *devours.*

"Your turn to smother him with your cum, *My Lady of Death,"* Jack sounds out quietly in my ear.

While his hands roam, cupping and squeezing my aching tender breasts, I can see so clearly how the two men watch each other. The tension becomes impalpable.

Roman's tongue wickedly laps me up, stroking and curling, flicking his tantalizing tongue against my clit. My mind is on the cusp of breaking again. It takes Jack's lips on mine to muffle my sounds.

These men are my dark paradise. My favorite place to be, and I'm already enjoying being between them.

My second orgasm hits me faster than the first. While I come apart, Jack's hand clamps my mouth shut as I cry out, relishing Roman's soft noises that bring music to my ears.

"A sexy sight, *both of you,"* Jack whispers while Roman licks his lips, standing.

My shaky legs can barely hold me up as Jack keeps his hold on me. Within a flash, Roman moves closer, claiming Jack's mouth right beside my head.

Fuck. Me.

They groan in unison as I turn my head and watch them in pure wonder. With the way they kiss, I can witness how hungry they are for one another, and it's perfection to see.

"You taste great on his lips," Ro declares delicately when Jack suddenly cups the back of his head, holding him close.

I can feel his cock pushing against his pants, both of them in the front and the back.

Ro does the same with one hand and uses the other to pull me closer, licking Jack's lip before moving to mine. All three of us share a kiss before using our tongues openly, switching from Jack to Roman and then to each other.

My insides are churning, the ache for them to fill me is agonizing, and finally, to see them break all their barriers.

"If all is successful with our little plan, I need you both to fuck me in celebration," I speak with heavy breaths.

They agree as I kiss them both ardently. I long for them both, but I require the motivation to get through the masquerade.

These next two weeks will be absolute torture.

YOUR STORY

Frail masculinity
    Unfurling within your insanity
    Can you see?
    Keep underestimating me

You shall see in time,
    On a whim or rhyme
    Undertaking your claim to what is mine

Given or taken
    I think you are mistaken
    Love your enemy
    Devour the words of many
    Understand me not,
    Surely, you are but an afterthought

For I do not think of you
    Unveil what you think to be true
    Remember it when you are blue

Restate your hate
    Or at midnight you will be late

Will I see you for all that you are?
    So it goes, I will never be far

— E.G. Poa

CHAPTER SIXTEEN

CAGED BY YOU

ROMAN

Jack and I steal everything from a nearby town to look our best for the masquerade. All of us come up with a clever theme, symbolizing our relationships with each other. He would don fancy red attire with an attached cape and a skull mask. *The Red Death.*

I choose more simply, a black tux with a caged metal lace mask, Venetian style. I attach a chain with a red ruby clipping onto the coat pocket. Subtle but secret to the three of us. Arde mentions a black dress and a raven mask for herself.

I can't wait to see her and Jackson in all their splendor. *And to finally have them.*

The past two weeks were...*rough.* All I could think about was fucking them. The torture coerced me into jacking off as often as I could when I was alone just to find some reprieve. It held me *only a little.*

There is radiating sexual tension between us when our Yellow Eyes isn't around. We agreed to wait until after the masquerade. *Unfortunately, for motivation purposes to get through it...*

I remembered the day in the library, kissing him after all these years, seeing him knelt between her thighs, tasting the divine while also looking my way.

The sexiest fucking sight.

Afterward, with our tongues tangling together, *I was so stiff.* The way he watched me as I took a turn between her legs, a silent promise reserved just for me.

I could've died right then.

Being with them felt like death should feel. Full of promise, unconditional love, and the bliss that comes with it. I would die happy if I could have them for the rest of my life. Complete and in utter serenity. My Little Raven had slowly corrupted me.

Arde had booked a fancy stay in a hotel without letting us contribute, knowing we used all our money to buy our new home. She also arranged transportation, figuring it would be best to arrive separately. Hence, our plan to incorporate red into our outfits somehow. Her chosen red piece will be a single satin red silk ribbon woven through her thickly braided hair, along with a red necklace of some sort.

The mystery is intriguing, and I can't wait to see who the fuck Prick Furrows will unveil himself to be. The masquerade event is being held in a swanky location at one of the large ballrooms in the city's largest building. I had never been, but Arde is more familiar with the city.

This night will be the first of many...

Nervousness begins settling in. I leave before Jackson in my own black car, and I'll be the first to arrive. I let my thoughts roam while I got ready earlier and on the way.

Now, it's time to focus.

Working my jaw at how much money she must have spent

has me flexing my fingers as I hold the mask in my hands during the ride.

All of us are wondering who Gildus Furrows is and if he's young enough to get his ass kicked. *For being a prick to My Little Raven, of course.*

During these past two weeks, Jack and Arde had gone over her creative works, explaining different meanings, along with Gildus's.

Her work is more romantic sounding, which is all I can remember. Sweet like a song. Maybe it's biased of me since I'm in love with her, but from what I can tell, Gildus doesn't give me or Jack any *feeling* from his words.

His went something like:

"One, two

Something in the dark is coming for you. To and fro,

Who I am you'll never know."

Or the best one.

"Love is blind, love is hate You are too late."

I *had* to make fun of him. What a fucking garden gnome. I can't wait to see what the bastard looks like. My fingers are itching to fuck him over somehow. Arde can win in wit and pretty words. I could...in *other* ways, like a simple punch to the face.

Part of me is glad we came up with a plan to protect her in case of some sort of scuffle, or violence of any kind occurring.

Over my dead body, though. Not on my watch, asshole.

Jackson can handle himself, and probably Arde too, but I can still protect them both. They are mine to do so with. *Thank God.*

Unclenching my jaw, I stare outside at the night sky beyond the window, my mind wandering until arriving.

Here we fucking go.

A black carpet stretches out on the sidewalk, leading into

the front double doors. A fancy sign hangs above: *The Masque of Unveiling.*

How fitting.

I secure my mask over my face, tying it behind my slicked-back hair.

Exhaling a deep breath, I step out as the cameras flash.

According to the news, it's the most anticipated event *ever*.

No one speaks to me as I make my way inside. There isn't a single person taking names to enter—anyone can walk in.

No matter to me, though.

Let's get this fucking party started.

The place is decorated in a dark, sultry fashion. Dark curtains and sensuous lighting with black chandeliers. It's perfectly classic in a way suited for my girl's morbidity. I know Arde will enjoy the décor; hell, I certainly do, and I'm just an asshole.

Everyone in the place wears all sorts of strange masks, ranging from animals to cages and bedazzling jewels on their faces. I also spot a few plague masks of varying colors. For the most part, people are in black, white, or red, plus a few blues and grays mixed into the crowd. The music itself is seductive, haunting even. It pricks my skin, setting the tone for what could await later that evening.

I seek out the bar, happy to find it's open—no money required, *bingo.*

After my first drink, I find myself on the open-level second floor that overlooks the main area. I lean on the railing to see if I can find my pale-haired raven or my *Red Death.*

The growing crowd comes to life with the dancing, moving their bodies and being close together as if awakened by the seduction the music brings. A few women look my way, undoubtedly intrigued by my interesting mask and attire. I feel like what I presume a rich man to be, exuding confidence, power, and secrets. Secrets of who the real E.G. Poa is.

I'm taken by two wonderful people, and I'm solely focused on them. Before Ardella, I would've entertained other women. However, I'm not that man anymore. Sex and money are not everything to me as it once was. Interestingly enough.

What matters is the two people I covet most.

I find Jackson in the crowd below before Ardella.

He appears as a passionate version of death, bathed in red.

His entrance has people turning heads and murmuring echoes throughout the room between the songs playing. My heart floods with how much I love him. How the anticipation of finally having him is killing me slowly. *He can be my red death and take me away after tonight.*

I have loved him for a long time.

Maybe it was his kindness in our youth, or that we shared a bedroom our whole lives, where I watched him become the perfection he is today.

The man himself strolls in as if he owns the place, and I'm nearly hard at the sight. At least on the second level view, no one can see me getting hard, not with the mood lighting anyway.

I watch him wander around as an upbeat song plays. He hasn't noticed me yet, but I get lost in watching him. My attention is solely on him until someone else enters my vision, drawing my attention away.

It's then that I see a beautiful vision stride through the front entrance. Stepping into motion, I make my way down the fancy stairs in the back part of the room.

It takes me longer than I care to admit to find her again in the crowd, but once I do, my breath catches in my throat, rendering me hopelessly speechless.

Before me stands my dark and beautiful little raven. Her black dress is long and flowy. There are lacey, high slits at each of her thighs. Lace crosses at her wrists and then at her shoulders—her arms bare. Her neckline is covered in lace, plunging low, revealing those delicious breasts, minus her nipples. Alluring and sensual. There's a small, red velvet bow tied around her neck, a black raven mask covering the top half of her face. Those yellow eyes are bright and perfect. Her hair is braided thickly behind her, revealing an interwoven red silk ribbon with luscious lips painted red.

I nearly kneel before her in worship. Fuck.

To entertain her, I bow, extending my hand.

"May I have this dance, My Little Raven?"

Kissing the top of her hand, I see her lips curl at the corner of her mouth, amused with me.

"I'd love to be caged by you."

A low grunt settles within as I lead her into the crowd, finding a place to pull her close and breathe her in. A sweet scent, *her scent.*

"I have no words for how mercilessly beautiful you are, how you seduce this entire room. The male in red is lingering in the back corner, biding his time... Fuck me, Arde," I groan in her ear, "you look so fucking edible. All mine—*ours.*"

"*Yours,*" she repeats, wrapping her arms around my neck while I hold her close, swaying to a slower song.

"You look delicious too, you know." Her eyes flicker as I take in her raven-masked face.

"You really do look sinfully perfect. I know Jackson is picturing our afterparty later," I lower my voice, tugging on her ear as she breathes out blissfully.

The song changes to something more seducing, and I begin our devilish dance.

"Hold on," I mention as I spin her around, leaning her down at an angle so that she's gazing up at me.

Her full leg is showing, so I run my hand up her thigh under the lace.

No fucking underwear—*fuck.*

I swear she does this shit on purpose.

Biting the inside of my cheek, I pull her up and spin her around again before we eye each other intently. She moves her body in slow, rhythmic motions that set fire to my blood, *my heart.*

Eyes are on us, but they keep dancing too, thankfully. I don't need a spectacle, just *her eyes on me.*

Those yellow eyes remain on me as I follow her around dancing and twirling, before capturing her into my Venetian cage. I see those red lips part, and with the way she's moving into me, she's also seducing me with her call of death. Gladly, I will follow her to it.

Angling my leg out, she straddles it, moving her hands to cup the back of my neck, eyes glazing over in lust. In a quick motion, we move together and against each other. We stay eye-locked, forgetting the rest of the people. I sneak a hand under, knowing she's wet as sin. When I find how soaked she is, I swipe two fingers slyly and bring them to my lips, adjusting the mask to do so.

She curses, turning around with her back to me, before I pull her flush against my chest, wrapping my arms around her waist. Leaning into her ear while we still move, I press my cock against her, so she feels what she does to me.

"This is what you have waiting for you after this is over. Filling you, making you come, over and over. Jack and I will make your dreams come true. I'm going to fuck you as you deserve, My Little Raven."

She rolls her body into me, grinding her hips as if she were making love publicly for all eyes to see.

"Can't wait," she breathes out, enticing me to move my hips with hers to the melodies dancing around us.

We lose ourselves in our sensuous lust, and the weight of her pressing tight against my cock is more than I can bear. I squeeze her ass and wish I could kiss the red off her lips.

After our sexy spectacle, I bring Arde to the bar, grabbing a round and clinking our drinks. Her beautiful smile instantly molds my heart with how free she appears under her raven mask. Knowing that we have her back and what awaits us, I lift my mask and angle my head to capture those red lips before we set out to find our Mr. Red Death.

CHAPTER SEVENTEEN

UNVEILED

JACK

Whoever this enemy would reveal themselves to be? I wonder about it as I stalk into the dark, sensual ballroom. People are everywhere in their dark fashions and masks.

Cloaked in red, I peer out of my skull mask, letting my eyes drift around to find Roman and Ardella. To my dismay, it takes me longer than I would have liked to find them.

It's the raven mask and something red woven through her hair that alerts me.

She steals the breath from my lungs as I draw closer. The way her black dress hugs her lithe, curvy body accentuates the very same planes of her that I adore. I can't wait until this night is over.

Roman is just as seducing in his Venetian metal lace mask, donning all black. A handsome dark prince. My poetic spirit can't take it; not the both of them together, ruining me forever at the same time.

For the past two weeks, all I could think about was Roman's

lips on mine and the visions of us together, entangling in limbs and sexy sighs. The wait is driving me crazy in my mental and sexual pandemonium.

Standing in the crowded room as I slowly make my way toward them, movements slow and blur as the two dance together. It reminds me of two stars colliding, making me fondly warm within.

The music becomes seductive in a slow, easy way. Seeing Ardella and Roman entwining in their own slow dance of sweet death. I can see it all so clearly as I observe them. The only two people in this crowd that I care about most; that *I love the most.*

The wait will be worth it. The minute his luscious lips wrap around my cock while Ardella observes, pleasuring herself at the sight of the two people she loves most... I will bask in Roman looking up beneath his lashes and watching me unravel. *Such a sweet death indeed.*

All three of us make an enticing pairing, and I can't wait to explore it thoroughly.

Just get through this masquerade unveiling in a few more hours.

The song finishes by the time I stand before them, smiling salaciously. "You both look... *I'm speechless and can't wait to have you two later...*"

My Lady of Death grins wickedly. It's hard to make out Roman's facial expression beneath his mask, but somehow, I can *feel* those eyes drinking me in. A silent promise—to devour so irrevocably.

He's my dark king, one I want to drop to my knees and worship down at his fucking altar, sucking him dry. Ardella gives me an amorous look as if envisioning what I see in my mind of all of us.

How the fuck will we get through the night?

"It's *my* turn to steal a dance. You both have the room hot and bothered," I tease.

I kiss the top of Ardella's hand as Roman and I switch places. Instead of both of them, my eyes focus solely on her. Her dress is even more tasteful up close. The exposure of skin, along with the sporadic lace and those breasts I crave to taste.

Yellow eyes watch me as I lead her to the center of the room, where the crowd is.

I need to put on a show.

I can feel all eyes on us. The guy in red and the mysterious beauty in black. My outfit is theatrical, to say so the least. A saccharine smile creeps upon Ardella's lips as I place a hand at her waist and then another gently in her hand.

"Ready to give this room a show?" I ask while the music changes into something spectacular.

A real ballroom *blitz*.

The instruments begin, and Ardella grins as we pick up our feet and move. We turn our heads fast from left to right quickly, making brisk work of our feet, and others begin to do the same. I take her for a spin when there's a break in the beat.

"She's the passionate one," the lyrics bounce around us.

When she spins back around to me, she takes the sides of her dress into her hands, showing even more leg; *it doesn't slip my notice.* She shimmies back and forth, moving closer as I sway my hips before holding my hand out to her and shaking my shoulders.

She's so goddamn sensual as she spins into my arms, then I rotate her so quickly, I worry I give her whiplash, but when she turns back to me as I take her hands into mine, I see she's more than fine.

She mouths the words to the song, *"Oh, yeah!"*

I can't keep my eyes off her as we come alive with the energy of the song and the masked people following suit. When it's over, I can't deny my disappointment. The energy emanating from us *is electric.*

Her laughter tickles my ears as I turn to her while she grips my hands tightly.

"My Masque of Red Death has the moves." Pulling her closer, I glance down.

"If this skull mask wasn't in my way, my tongue would be down your throat," I tell her, catching her alluring eyes twinkling with delight.

"Save it for me later, *My Death.* I suspect the reveal will be soon."

I touch her arm with a gentle caress in response.

"Slow dance with me?" I hold out my hand in invitation as she takes it with a smile.

Her hands go to my shoulders and mine to her hips once more.

"Are you nervous for the reveal, like I am?" Her words are faint, but I can somehow hear them over the music.

"No. Nothing to fear with your... what are *we* to you anyway?" I'm slightly teasing her, but I'm partially serious on the same token.

Her eyes remain like glue to mine. "Isn't it obvious?"

Knowing the answer, I tease, moving my hand to cup her ass. "This ass is mine, *yes,* but what about your soul? Your heart?"

Yellow eyes burn bright as she stares, her mouth falling open slightly.

In a sultry tone, she answers me as I expect, "I guess you'll see my soul later when you both tear me apart... When I'm filled to the brim, only then will I share where my heart is."

Tease.

Her eyes show the answers to all my questions. We are tired of waiting, yet we need to prepare for tonight without distractions. After the library instance with all three of us, I knew it would be all we'd crave. With the stress of her career, her missing father and brother, and her sister's passing, we didn't want sex to deter from the goal of the reveal. *Her protection from whoever the face is behind Gildus Furrows.*

Neither of us have said *the words,* but it doesn't mean we don't *feel* them. It shows in each of our actions where our hearts and minds are with one another. We see a future, and we *are* together. The professions of love would soon follow, I'm sure.

Initially, it was physicality, but it only heightened the addiction to her. Our fascination with the morbid creature with yellow eyes. Her intelligent, kissable mouth and her delicious cunt—what else would Roman and I ever need? *Except the crossing of the final line with each other.*

Now that I know he feels the same, it takes everything within me for self-restraint.

Soon.

I will fuck them both *real* soon.

Before I knew how much time had passed, the lights flicker and the music eases to a complete stop.

Some white-masked man spoke loudly about how it was nearing midnight. *The masque unveiling will happen shortly.*

I smirk, wondering where Ro wandered off to, when the man himself suddenly appears at our side.

"Ready?" He looks from me to Ardella.

I hear her heavy sigh as I nod, saying nothing for a few minutes until the room is too dim to see.

"Stay close to the grand stairs so you can see who it is," I mention quietly before disappearing into the crowd, biding my time.

At the stroke of midnight, the bell echoes from the cathedral nearby so loud and eerie that I feel it vibrate deep within my bones. Energy in the room is fickle and tense as the lights flicker back to their original allure.

The same, white-masked gentleman stands between two sets of elegant staircases with a set of steps with white marble below him.

A crowd gathers near the stairs. Low whispers create a static noise, like the sound of a heartbeat colliding with rising anticipation. Lifting their masks up, the people clap.

The guy, assuming it's Ardella's boss, goes on to explain the excitement of two writers who battled the column pages and magazines for years.

Just who are Gildus and E.G.?

Another gentleman in a matching black mask, the opposing side to be presumed, shakes the other guy's hand. Both men are older with blonde, silvery hair. Despite the enemy writers they hosted, the two males seem friendly.

The guy in the black mask, after lifting it from his face, calls for Gildus to step forward first.

Of course, they save the best for last.

An entire crowd waits anxiously. All there is silence while people look around curiously. The pause is the worst part, seemingly dragging on the midnight show.

Shoes clack on the floor from the far side of the room, making their way up to the grand staircases where the two men in charge stood. *So mysterious and cliché.*

A dark-haired gentleman in all black with a golden animal mask, antlers protruding from the top, steps from the lurking shadows of the pillars.

The guy walks up the steps, silent as night. He appears younger, but I could be mistaken with the mask.

Then, Ardella's boss, the one with the white mask, calls E.G. forward.

I let them wait and stew in the silence longer than *Gildus.*

A few heartbeats linger before I slowly make my way from the side I stand at which is opposite from the enemy's side.

Gasps ring out as I ascend the flight of stairs. The two bosses clap as Gildus glares. The closer I get, I realize Gildus has sapphire blue eyes.

Standing on the other side of *my* boss, he shakes my hand with a shit-eating grin, clapping my shoulder.

"Gentlemen, off with the masks!" Both speak in unison as Gildus and I face each other.

His is off before mine, and I take my time, drawing it out just to spite him. I can see his glare as I do.

The guy would be handsome enough if he wasn't such an asshole to the *real* E.G. Poa.

Once I'm entirely unveiled, I see him taking me in, too. The wheels appear to be turning in his self-entitled, cruel mind. I keep my face blank as we simply stare at each other.

Then, a familiar voice echoes at the front of the crowd, "Are you fucking kidding me?"

E.G. POA

CHAPTER EIGHTEEN

GILDUS FURROWS

ARDELLA

"Are you fucking kidding me?"

Gildus Furrows...is *Rigswold?*

What in the *absolute fuck* of fucks!

Roman tugs on my hand as I stand frozen.

The world tilts off its axis as he moves to stand behind me to keep me upright. My knees feel like they're going to give out underneath me. *Thank fuck for the raven mask.*

Jackson hears me, along with a few other people, but Rigs is too focused on glaring at Jack before sneering.

"Arde, who is that?" I hear Roman whisper as my boss and his friend speak to the crowd for applause while the men glare at each other in a silent battle of staredowns.

"*It's my fucking ex,*" I get out gravelly, trying to steady my racing heart.

Because, of course, it's him.

I hear his growl despite the claps and cheers echoing. Suddenly, *Rigs* turns towards the crowd, his face adjusting from a scowl to one of shock upon seeing me. The only one in the crowd with raging yellow eyes.

"I need some air, Ro. Please don't follow me."

He reluctantly releases me from his hold as Rigs starts towards me, and soon Jack is following behind him, probably not understanding the situation yet.

I turn and bolt through the crowd, ignoring my name being called.

No, no! Why him?

After getting turned around various hallways, I find myself in a courtyard between buildings. The night air is calming enough as I take the deepest breath, letting it fill my lungs and my broken heart.

What even is my life right now?

Not only did he get engaged to another woman, but he was my archnemesis too? The universe *really* liked to fuck me over.

I try to shake out my impending panic and racing thoughts. A large gazebo stands at the center with dark plants and flowers in baskets around it. Romantic lighting decorates the place. I would've appreciated it more if my thoughts weren't jumbled.

Thankfully, I'm alone to grip the railing on the gazebo to get myself more together. I take off my mask and throw it to the grass in frustration.

The breeze blows gently, giving rise to another chill. There was power beneath my mask. Now, I'm exposed and vulnerable. It had nothing to do with the point of that night. Did he honestly not know it was me?

"Ardella," a voice echoes in the darkness.

I spin around to see him, the *last* person I want to see. My heart speeds up as he steps onto the gazebo platform with me.

"God, I haven't seen you in *years,* and you're just as beautiful as the last time I saw you." His hand reaches towards my face, but I move away, my back to him.

"Why are you here with him? My enemy?" I can hear how upset he is...

With an *audacity* that I should care.

Huffing a bitter laugh, I tell him, "I saw you before in the city when I was in school. *You're engaged to a woman who looks like me.* How was I supposed to know who you were in disguise? Looks like both sides wanted anonymity..." I shake my head at such absurdities of fate. "But you..."

My eyes water while Rigswold sighs, and I hear him inching toward me more, closer than I'm comfortable with.

"I—"

Interrupting him, I snap, "I don't want to hear your excuses. Why didn't you ever come back?"

Spinning around, I find him *so much closer.*

"I made a mistake..."

He grabs my face, forcing me to look at him. I struggle in his grasp as he holds my face. The tears slide down my cheeks.

"Haven't we all? You looked pretty happy to me. Why bother with the depressing mortician girl for the rest of your life? When opportunities are endless for you? Save your breath, Rigs, don't waste it on me. You haven't come around for years, so spare me further heartache I've held onto for far too long already. You were my first love... Not my last. I've had enough for one evening. *I'm* your enemy."

He drops his hands in defeat, shaking his head. "You are not my enemy. *He is. He also has you.*"

I step back, scoffing. The feud is more important to him.

Shouldn't be so surprised.

"It will always be *me.* He isn't the only one that has me... I have two men I love very much, and they feel the same."

I try to get away again, but he grabs my arm tighter this time.

"Ardell—"

I halt, giving him the side eye, ready to flee or fight him immediately.

"Remove your hand from her before I remove it for you. *Now.*"

Chills spread through me at the sound of Roman's authoritative voice.

A glance in the direction of his voice, and the man himself steps out of the shadows cloaked like death coming to claim a life.

"Who the fuck are you?" Rigs asks, loosening his grip but not letting go.

As if he had any authority to demand anything.

"I haven't been yours since we were kids, Rigs... Let go of me before I cause a scene." I work my jaw, irritated as hell.

Jackson comes out of the shadows too ready to reap.

"Touch her again, *Rigsy,* and we'll have a serious problem. Death wouldn't even save you from my wrath."

Roman's words make me wet as Rigs releases me. I've never been defended like this before, and *it's a delight.*

Relieved to see them both, I make my way out from under the gazebo and into Ro's arms, seeking solace in his heat of passion and anger.

He looks me over, making sure I'm unharmed. A tear drops from my eye. Jack leans in to catch it with his finger and moves past us towards Rigs.

"I should kill you for making her cry, you *bastard.*"

Roman cups my face and kisses my forehead. The gesture fills me with warmth, thawing the ice in my heart that once was. That Rigs keeps leaving me with, digging my grave over and over.

The man himself laughs. "I should kill you. You don't deserve her, and I hope you don't embarrass yourself with those words you publish that *you* call creativity. Don't make me laugh."

He sounds bitter that I'm with them, but he has *no fucking right*.

"Like yours are any better? I cry myself to sleep, I'm so bored!"

Rigs laughs again, the gesture taunting the men around me. "I agree with him. I die of boredom with every line I read of yours. So unfeeling and unpassionate in comparison, *Rigsby*."

Roman stands in front of me, shielding me behind him as he walks up next to Jack.

"It's Rigswold!"

My smirk grows. I move behind Roman to lean my head into his back and place my hand on Jack's waist.

"Riggy, Rigsby, Rig—I don't care what your name is. You're fucking pathetic. Although, I can see the appeal of you back then to her... Now, all I see is an entitled asshole."

I hear a bunch of grunts and growls then. *A dick measuring contest.*

Stepping between the two men, I face my men, both aroused and flattered by their heated gazes, evaporating me further into a puddle of their heroic love.

"Alright, the pissing contest is over. Let's go. I have nothing else to say except this..." I turn around toward Rigs, the lights dancing all around, illuminating him in a way that makes him look like a great betrayer. A fallen angel, perhaps.

My hands are out beside me disabling Jack and Ro from stepping forward to pummel Rigswold. *Part of me wouldn't mind witnessing such a spectacle.*

"Between you and I, Rigswold, *I* am your enemy because he's not the true writer here, although he certainly speaks another language with that tongue of his..."

Jack leans into me, kissing the top of my head in appreciation of how I threw those luscious words out without a care.

"*I* am E.G. Poa, and you've broken my heart for the last fucking time, Rigswold. I am done with you, forever. I will not find you, even in death. You are no lover of mine, not like them."

He looks conflicted, wounded even, but I continue.

"I don't want to see you again. Do not drag my name through the papers and let this be the end of this little...*feud.* Go back to your wife. Goodbye, Rigswold."

I give him one last look, my heart pooling at my feet like bloody goop from the grand reveal of my enemy, and usher my men back to the building. They look hesitant, but thankfully, nothing else happens. Rigs only stands there, watching us leave with the heartache written all over his face.

Fuck you, Gildus Furrows. Your power is gone now.

The further we walk back to the ongoing party, somehow, peace settles within me that I left telling him who the real enemy is.

Let him come for me after this, I dare him. I'll bury him.

"Are you ready to leave this place, or do you want to dance with us both?" Jack asks from beside me once we make it back to the main ballroom.

"We don't need to hide anymore... I need a drink after all of that. Let's dance for a little while before we leave," I tell them, making my way to the bar.

They say nothing, and we slam drinks down before meandering into the drunk dancing crowd. I hear multiple people stop to tell Jackson how they admire his work. My heart stitches back together at the words.

Roman, to no one's surprise, pulls me closer first. "Are you okay, little raven?"

Appreciating his fun nicknames as I always do, I shake my head.

"No, but I will be, eventually. The shock of it...still has me reeling. What a prick."

"Agreed, *fucking Prick Furrows*." His eyes search mine, pausing briefly to reach up and caress my cheek. "When I saw him grabbing you... I saw red."

My heart flies off into the sunset. At this rate, with how in love with them I am, I'd start writing about rainbows and flowers.

"You aren't the only one," I hear Jackson say from behind me as he leans his chin on my shoulder, looking at Roman. "Hearing you defend us was something, though," he adds.

Holding my breath, Roman speaks, "You love us, huh?"

"You heard all that, hmm?" I dare to ask, exhaling my held breath.

"And apparently, we feel the same?" He tilts that handsome face of his, catching Jack's eyes.

My heart drops.

"Yeah, so you assumed it, hmm?" Jack adds softly in my ear. Feeling confused by their reactions, I begin to stutter.

"I was just telling him things so he'd back off... I'm sorry for assuming—"

Roman puts his finger to my lips. "That asshole didn't deserve the time of day. We should've been the ones to hear it *first*."

I sigh. Roman is right. *For once.*

"I'm sorry—"

Jack's finger goes over my lips next to shush me. "It's too late now," Jack says into my ear.

I spin around, ready to say something, when Jack pulls me to him, tipping my chin up.

"For what it's worth, Ardella, I'm hopelessly in love with

you. Until death do I part from you. You are *not* the depressing mortician girl. Every breath spent with you is precious, and don't you ever let anyone make you feel less than what you are. You are *my death,* ensnaring me in this life. So beautifully and tragically so, you are stuck with me, My Morbid Angel."

Tears fill my eyes as I smile at him, my heart swooning over his precious words.

"You are just as morbid to put up with my antics and poetics," I tell him before he kisses me deep and slow.

Moaning into him, I can't believe I had to wait all night to kiss them both.

When we finally pull away, my lips tingle in the wake of it. I whisper, *"I love you."*

His eyes shine in appreciation and love, and tears gather in them. We finally have our special moment. *Now, I need to give the same to Roman.*

I lightly caress Jackson's cheek before turning to Ro.

"I'm sorry you weren't the first ones to hear the words directly," I tell him as soft music plays around us.

He reaches for the bow I made with my velvet necklace and loosens it, pulling me closer to merge our lips.

We groan, and his hand cups my ass, squeezing briefly before pulling away to peer deep into my dark spirit.

"Jackson has a better way with words than I do, but all of it is true. There's nothing wrong with the weird and unordinary. Who cares about all of that? Fuck that guy for making you question your worthiness which is worth more than all the precious gems stolen for a better life. You are the better life, Arde. You are mine. I am yours. We are ours. All of us. I, your personal stalker, watching you in the moonlight, captivated even then. I fucking love you. I'm not worthy of you like Jacky is, but damn if I won't try for the rest of my life to be someone worthy."

I cup his cheek, appreciating his words equally. How could my heart be so broken but so full?

"You are worthy, Roman, and don't ever think otherwise. I love you, and you deserve all the love."

"From both of us," Jack steps in, and they exchange a look that makes me warm inside.

Leaning into Jackson, I place my hand on Roman's chest, rubbing the center of it as Jack kisses my head.

We whisper our *I love you's* as the music picks up.

"Fuck what we came here for. Let's dance. We have *love* to celebrate." I grin at them.

Suddenly, I'm being pressed between them, catching their hungry gazes aiming not only at me, but at each other. My pussy aches in wait, thrilled for the near future of long awaited sexual promises.

I know they want to dance with each other, but they are hesitant to do so in public, so instead, they turn me around, taking turns teasing and kissing me.

Drunk off them, I bask in their roaming hands and lingering kisses with soft, sensual touches.

They are all mine. To love and cherish.

Now, I get to fuck them both with all passion in my heart.

CHAPTER NINETEEN

EVERY CELL

ROMAN

"That cunt is mine," I whisper in her ear, pulling her into the elevator Jack is already waiting in so we can head to our fancy hotel room.

"What will we do with her first, Ro?" Jack asks suggestively, those gorgeous blue and green eyes haunting my soul. As they have for all these years.

The two weeks of waiting were already bad enough, and after the events of the evening—*enough is enough.*

"I know," she draws out in a hint, her chest rising in quick breaths as I pin her to the back wall of the elevator, "a promise you need to fulfill... Let me watch you both for the first time. *Please.*"

Those yellow eyes linger on my lips before meeting my brown-eyed gaze.

With my hands steady on either side of her head, I rather enjoy the way she squirms impatiently as I side-eye Jack. The man himself already has a darkening gaze full of desire. Those bright blues and greens swirl into a seducing dance of temptation.

As the elevator dings, I toss him a sneaky smirk signaling our floor.

"I have just the thing for you, Arde." I kiss her cheek, stepping away while Jack takes her hand.

She and Jack lead the way as I step aside to hear her giggle after Jack kisses her cheek.

Once we're down the end of the hall, she unlocks the room. The room we enter is enormous. Fancy in décor with names of styles I can't name, nor do I care to. Jack's cock is at the forefront of my mind, and where I crave him at the edge of my lips.

Lust drives me to the edge of what little thread I'm hanging by.

"Strip down, Jack, while I tie up our morbid girl here," I tell him with a wicked smile, leading Arde to the four poster king-sized bed.

Jesus Christ, how much did she spend on this place? There's even a big walk-in tub for all of us—*a note to use it later.*

I undo my black tie and take off my suit jacket and vest. My Little Raven jumps into bed with her dress still on, squealing in delight as I climb over her.

"I'm going to restrain you, Yellow Eyes. Is that okay with you?"

"Yes, *please.*" She sounds like a little sex kitten.

With a side smirk, I lean down and whisper, "Hmm, so she's secretly a *good* little morbid girl, after all."

She breathes out as I ask Jack for his red tie. I use mine to tie one of her wrists to one side of the post and end up using his for her other wrist once he tosses it to me.

"Before we get started with your show, let me see how wet you are," I murmur, trailing light kisses down the center of her breasts, pulling up her dress.

"Are the restraints okay?" Jack asks quietly as she nods.

He's nude beside the bed and my mouth waters. *Fuck, he's a sight to behold. Just as I already knew from growing up together.*

Once her bare pussy appears from under the dark fabric, I settle my face between her thighs, tasting her essence with a groan of approval.

"And?" Jack inquires, crawling into bed and leaning close to her face.

"She's so fucking wet." I keen my satisfaction.

"Good."

He kisses her while I kiss her other lips, sliding my tongue up and down her slit, purring at the hot, wet taste of her. *We* do it for her, and it's enough to keep me stiff, aching for our final entanglement at last.

Looking up from my position between her thighs, I see Jack kneading her breast with her tongue down his throat. A sly smile crosses me, and I slip two fingers inside her to stroke her inner walls. They tighten at my intrusion while I hear a sweet moan release above me.

"Come here, Jack," I say softly, beckoning him as I kiss her inner thigh before sitting up on my knees while keeping my fingers inside her.

My thumb circles her clit. "Let her watch as she comes for the first time tonight, of many more to come, when you kiss me," I say as he kisses her long and slow before pulling away and moving toward me.

"Good thinking, Ro," his words shoot to my groin; her noises grow louder with my fingers working her inner muscles.

Behind me, he aids in taking off the rest of what I'm wearing on the top half of my body, his lips following from my neck to my shoulders once they're bare to him. I shiver, enjoying his attention *finally.*

"Your turn to tease her while I tease you." He tugs on my ear in silent agreement.

We switch spots, and it's amusing how Ardella seeks more friction, squirming when my fingers leave her.

I quickly take off my pants, my cock springing free. I press against his gorgeous backside, letting my lips trace the same space he found on me moments ago. His skin smells good, fresh citrus from his earlier shower.

"You're right. Look how wet she is. *All for us.*"

I nibble on his neck as he tenses slightly but relaxes. Having him so close to me skin-to-skin is more than I can bear. I'm aching for him; *for her, too.*

No more waiting.

Reaching my hand around to his lower abdomen, I grip the base of him before tugging a few times. He leans into me, sighing as he fingers our girl. She's tugging on the restraints, moaning and losing herself over her pleasure and ours. Her eyes flutter open and close, trying to bask in her pleasure and by watching her two favorite men. *The men she loves.*

I bask in that knowledge as I let the myriad of sensations wash over me–him, me, and her. Soon, we will be full of each other. A separate three before merging to one. One love, one heart, one death—all of us connected.

I stroke him, holding him steady with my body, my dick resting against his ass. I run my fingers through his hair, and his head eases back for me with a beautiful moan leaving his lips. His decadent sounds will be my undoing. I'm already heightened in my senses. My skin is highly alert to his against mine. His body, so full of strength, so beautiful, is all in my grasp, giving everything to me.

With my lips on the skin of his neck, I glance down toward My Little Raven, her eyes rolling back as she comes apart for the first time. Jack moves his hand up to cup my head, angling his face to meet my lips.

"Let me feel your lips," he mutters.

Smiling against his lips, I release my hold on his cock, and we adjust ourselves on the bed. He leans against one of the posts near Arde's legs as I lay down, angling myself so she can see. I wet my lips, giving him a lustful look that tears a grunt from his throat.

I cup his balls, placing my mouth over his head, slick with pre-cum. Toying with him at first, I curl my tongue, teasing him with the tip of it. His soft sighs are riveting until I feel his hand in my hair, scrunching his fingers in. Eager for his reaction, I take him fully into my mouth, gagging slightly with him down my throat.

Ardella curses as I suck his engorged cock. I'm practically mewling in our pleasures and moaning with him; much to my delight, he begins to fuck my mouth, and I lose myself there. His salty taste is all I want and more, when he warns me he's going to come.

Watching him fall apart because of me fuels our rendezvous forward. I'm lost in him and in how Ardella watches us enthusiastically. To my surprise, I don't gag as he spills down my throat, filling me with that hot cum.

"Fuck me, Jackson."

When he agrees, I realize I didn't think about it inwardly.

I make a satisfying noise, sitting up as he takes a deep breath and pulls me to meet his lips.

"What about you?" He peers into my brown eyes, reaching for my own aching dick.

"We have all night. I've been waiting to feel you... *Please.*" A silent plea that I'm desperate for him.

With his answering kiss, I draw him out of bed.

"Let's release our girl, so she can join in," he suggests, and we watch her eyes widen, lips parting before she tucks her bottom lip between her teeth.

We go on either side of her, undoing the ties, and she relaxes in relief.

"You two are a sight behold," she says honestly, and I tuck some of her hair behind her ear as she sits up.

"Having you watch is something new," Jack adds, leaning over to steal a kiss from her while I take her hand and kiss the top.

"Seeing you on all fours, Little Raven, now, wouldn't *that* be something."

She narrows her gaze but smiles while moving toward me, getting on all fours.

"My pussy is yours to use as you will. *Both* of you."

Both of us growl in agreement, my throat vibrating with such a demand.

We most certainly will.

Jack crawls into bed behind her, licking her ass before going further south, lapping at her pussy.

The sight is sinful as she takes me into her mouth with that expert tongue of hers that I already know so intimately well. I rustle as she licks down the thick length of my cock. Watching how she enjoys herself while closing her eyes, I run my hand through her pale locks, undoing her fancy braid until her hair spills down all curly, tossing the red ribbon elsewhere.

I decide to take the view of him in. Jack is enjoying her with shut eyes. Our moans are creating a symphony of deliciousness. I begin to swell more with an upcoming frantic release. Her low purring sounds are my undoing as I fuck her mouth to the finish. With a low rumble, I spill down her throat. My good Little Raven sucks out every last drop until I shiver.

My heart races as my mind reels how we're all together like

this. Pure nirvana entombs me when I slip out of her mouth to claim those greedy lips of hers, tasting myself on her tongue.

"Where should we fuck you first, little raven?" I graze my lips against hers, those eyes half lidded as she releases a soft cry, closing her eyes at Jack's sinful tongue.

"I'm already back here, Ro, fuck *me* first."

I meet his lively eyes, passion pooling in them so much I crave to swim in them for the rest of my life. Both of them. I need *both* for the rest of my life.

"I suppose," I hum in consideration, "bring that sexy ass to the edge of the bed for me."

He gives me a haughty look, pulling not only himself back, but Arde. I walk around the bed. It would be another minute or so before my dick would be ready to go again. Before he positions her entrance, I steal his lips, tasting our Lady Death on his tongue. We remain like this until I'm hard again, pulling away.

"I've never done this before, Jack. Please let me know if I hurt you," I whisper with a quick caress to his face, kissing his shoulder and neck before moving down his spine.

I admire such a backside. The strong muscles from digging graves and carrying my weight around all these years, he is utterly handsome and *all mine*. My first male, my only, *and* my last.

"I trust you, Ro." His voice is its own caress while he slips inside our woman who has a lovely backside of her own.

His words reach me deep as I kneel behind him and nibble on that perfect ass of his. Their moans get me going as I lick his rim thoroughly, preparing him.

"Wait, turn me around. I want to see you both as you come," Arde says, and I love her more for it.

"Very well," Jack flips her over and spreads her open before diving back inside her.

She's at an angle since Jackson is on all fours. Her feet are near my face, and I kiss the top of her foot.

"Lean forward slightly, Jacky," I tell him as he does, taking her legs under his arms and moving them towards her.

Spreading his ass cheeks, I play with his rim, stretching him slowly with my slick fingers. I take great care, making sure my fingers are soaked and wet before slipping them inside him. I wonder if his moans are from Arde or me as I continue to work inside him, feeling him stretch and adjust to my intrusion.

"Is this okay, Jack?" I ask softly, and he moans out, *"Yes."*

I spit down onto my cock, several times, working it in until it's slick, warning him ahead of time. Arde is already losing herself while I play.

"Are you okay, Jacky?" He begins to sound like he isn't enjoying himself, and I start to worry.

"Fuck, don't stop, Ro. Use that cock I have yet to taste."

Oh, those strangled sounds were of pleasure then... Hmm, well, how could I say no to that?

Groaning to myself, I stand tall and ensure my cock is still slick before easing myself into his tight channel. He goes stiff before I coax him sweetly into relaxing for me.

"Goddamn, you're so fucking tight," I tell him while placing my hands on his hips once I'm buried within.

An unholy sound leaves his handsome, kissable lips when I begin to thrust slowly.

"God, you feel amazing, Roman. So many wonderful sensations—fuck *me*," he says breathlessly.

A cute laugh leaves me as I do as he requests, seeing how Arde's eyes are in the back of her head, her mouth parting and panting with Jack's pacing. All of us are finally together, and it's heaven on earth.

"Lean against me and pull her so her legs are at your shoulders. I want to hold you both," I manage to get out somehow despite being lost in sinful sensations.

I couldn't fucking wait until it was my turn to let him take me.

Jack leans against me, and I wrap my arms around him and Arde's legs.

"You're so fucking perfect, Jackson, *so fucking perfect.*" I suck on his earlobe.

His grunts and moans turn into less tortured sounds and more into a sanctuary of bliss. Arde cries out not too long afterward, arching herself up with her head falling back, and Jackson joins her as he tightens around me. All it takes is for them to come apart for me to follow suit. I suck on his neck hard as if to lay my claim on him officially like some vampire.

"Fuck!"

Mm, Jacky Boy. My Jackson.

With all of us breathless and spent, I muster up some energy to ease out of him, plopping down next to Arde, heavily breathing at such lustful exertion.

Jack gently eases out of her pretty pink pussy, placing her legs down. He lay on the opposite side of her, those perfect eyes transfixed on me.

Arde looks between us before kissing us both.

"Brief intermission before...other rounds," she declares as I huff a laugh.

I lay my head on the crook of her neck.

"I love you both," I admit honestly, finding that love isn't the right word to describe how liberating and free I am with them.

My soul knows theirs, so wholly and completely. The strings of life and death are woven through us; their hearts and bodies are *mine.* Every cell in my body lives for them, fueling me to thrive alongside them. All of me, belonging to them for the rest of my miserable existence. However, *now*, it's not so miserable.

E.G.POA

CHAPTER TWENTY

OF ALL THEY GAVE

ARDELLA

I wake tangled in limbs. In the center of them, I lay in a bed large enough for all of us to stretch out comfortably. Roman is curled up behind me as Jack has me tucked into his chest, but his arm drapes across me, landing on Ro's side.

Never in my dreams did I expect to feel the way I do at that very moment. A sense of nirvana is shaping me into a new, unidentified form.

The distraction of the *Unveiling Masque Ball* kept me from spiraling about my missing father and brother and the tragedy of my sister's death. Hell, even my mother's from watching her turn into a ghost year after year. Tragedy felt like a family gathering, a curse.

How could I beat it? Death is all I know.

Somehow, I knew the answers lie on either side of me, encompassing me with their warmth and strength. Our attraction was fast like wildfire, aching to be touched and fucked. Yet somehow *more*.

In my mind, there was nothing wrong with being selectively promiscuous. I didn't just open my legs to everyone. *The mental attraction is what matters to me.* College did aid in that with the parties Anabel and I went to, where orgies took place, and I found the beauty of voyeurism and exhibitionism. All thanks to Ana.

I'd get on my knees like a good little whore if the other person enraptured me enough. I didn't *initially* do it with these men on either side of me. Their good looks were enough to capture my eyes but not superficial enough to be all I sought. They undressed my mind, letting me peer deeper. The banter with Roman got me hot and bothered, but I wouldn't give him the satisfaction then.

Now?

It's so much fun.

As I lay between them, I let my mind wander about major events and the blow of heartache that my sworn enemy is *Rigswold.* He acted *so* lovestruck but never once came back to visit or check-in. I was only convenient for him to pass the time with. He thought he could get that back with sweet, false lines and empty words. He *never* apologized sincerely, although I'm not sure I'd even believe him if he did. Words without actions are simply *that*: empty words with baseline, half-assed actions. Can't forget he's probably married too.

Maybe *fate* was trying to tell me something. How *Gildus* revealed a destiny that wasn't meant for me like I once yearned for. Along with the bitterness last night left me, something else lingers.

What happens next? What does the future hold for me now?

I know I'll need to seek out help for the funeral home since I can't do it by myself. I will write to my one true friend and dorm mate, *Anabel Lee*. The yin to my yang. Hopefully, her troubles aren't as woesome as mine...

I stir slightly, running my hand up Jack's side in a gentle stroke of my fingers. My mind is a jumbled mess, but I no longer feel so alone.

Before, I didn't mind the loneliness; it was ingrained in me, just like embalming and taking care of the dead before being laid to rest formally. A planned routine in a chaotic world trapped in Morella.

It didn't bother me before until I was the only one left in that house.

Distracting from my rising fear, Jack kisses the top of my head. Roman's hand tightens around me before poking me with his morning wood.

Smiling slyly to myself, I steal Jack's lips. It is then I take in his messy-haired look and sleepy bedroom eyes. He is a sight to behold as the late morning rays of light stretch across our skin, reminding me to cherish this perfect moment with them.

"I don't want to leave this bed," he mumbles sleepily, gazing down at me.

"Me either," Roman agrees, sounding half asleep.

"We don't have to do anything; we have the rest of the day. There's no checkout time today," I whisper as Roman's hand slowly caresses my hip.

"Someone's second brain is awake already," I tease while pushing my hips back as he thrusts forward, a low groan escaping him while he moves his hand down between my thighs.

"It's also *my first* brain, not second," Roman chides playfully, and Jack appears bemused before my mouth goes slack as Roman's fingers work my slit rising up to my clit.

"Nothing like a perfect morning with my lovers," Jack says while releasing his hold from around Ro and me.

"You're wet, My Little Raven... Why don't you roll over and let me give you a *proper* good morning?" Roman practically purrs into my ear as I release a soft sigh.

"Open up that delicious ass for me," Jack mentions before stealing a quick kiss.

I tingle at the prospect of them filling me. I toss a fiendish look to Jack before rolling over, and Roman pulls me atop him.

"There's our Death Angel," the fondness echoes from Roman as I bend down to suck on his tongue.

Good thing we slept nude.

My hair spills down, the light rays catching through the window, painting a sensual picture of artistry. Nudity and moans. We sigh out blissfully in unison the second I sink fully onto that glorious cock.

"You are so beautiful in the light," he says, and I lean back and ride him slowly and steadily, waking myself up more and more with the stretch and feel of him.

Relishing in it after getting thoroughly fucked only hours before, I close my eyes, enjoying the soreness and pleasure.

Roman's strong hand cups my breast before beginning to tease the peaks with his fingers. At the same time, Jack positions himself behind me, turning my head to the side and greeting me with another long kiss.

After watching the two men take each other at different sexual rounds hours ago, it brought me joy to see their love for each other shine through, and how they let me love them in return. An interesting dynamic, but one without complaints. It's all I ever dreamed about. Love amidst my entombment.

The love radiates between all of us. A flame to a piece of wintery ice is what they felt like, and I always crave to wrap myself in their cocoon. These two men made me feel so loved and cherished, and I hoped I could return the same of all they gave me.

CHAPTER TWENTY-ONE

SHE WOULD BE OUR DEATH

JACK

My lips move from hers, whispering for her to lean forward on Roman.

With my cock at attention as she does, I eat out her ass, preparing her for me. When she begins to writhe under me, I enter her tight hole.

Just as I did to Roman hours ago.

I've loved him far longer than I admitted, yet Ardella is included in that love.

Feeling him was all I imagined it would be, with so much pleasure and stimulation; it was a wonder how I didn't blow my load immediately as I fucked Ardella. As we came that first time, I stood firm in my resolve.

I will never let either of them go for as long as I breathe. My Lady Death and my *cocky* foster brother are now my lovers. Three separate people merging as one entity finally complete in all of our shared breaths in this life.

The past twelve hours were a first for all of us. A thing of sanctimonious dreams turned into a sinful reality, one I will be laid to rest in.

When I slip inside her tight channel, I groan as she tenses slightly before encouraging me to keep going. I can feel Roman inside our woman, and the sensation makes me feel closer than ever, my eyes rolling toward the back of my skull.

Gripping her hips, I ease in fully. With Roman's cock inside, I nearly come at the sensation, incredulous and all consuming. My eyes eventually open to a view of them lip-locked. Smirking to myself, I wrap her hair around my first and ease her back to me. I notice Roman's lustful brown eyes flick to me before his eyes close in sweet agony. *He feels me, too.*

Sucking on her neck, she arches her back while I increase my pace.

"This ass is mine," I growl out in a low timbre.

Before I know it, Roman is sitting up and wrapping those manly arms around us both, burying his head in her breasts.

She leans fully into me while we keep our pacing. Tugging on her earlobe, Ardella begins to tighten around me and Roman. He grunts, catching my gaze and squeezing my ass. Utmost desire fuels me, and as if thinking the same thoughts, we move our faces over her shoulder to steal a lavishing kiss.

Delighting in us, Ardella kisses us both before a cry leaves those precious lips. Taking my load in at the same time, Roman follows suit, biting her breast to stifle his finishing cry.

Seeing them both shatter is enough to satisfy me as we ease down from our high.

"Fuck," I groan out, easing my cock from her warmth and kissing her shoulder.

Moving towards the bathroom for a towel to clean ourselves off, I return to the room moments later to see them hugging each other in the same position.

Watching them with a deep fondness, I clean myself as she

moves from him, inching closer to me and taking the towel to do the same.

"Shall I prepare the bath for us? Might as well enjoy the luxury, right," she quips, a grin breaking the surface.

"Right behind you," I tell her as Roman agrees, moving toward me.

His eyes hold their intent as he moves in, stealing my lips and cupping my face in his hands to deepen it. The man takes my breath away, and when he pulls away, I reach for him again to return the favor.

When I feel him smirk, I pinch his ass.

"Being inside her at the same time might be my new favorite activity," he says with his glossy brown eyes that remind me of the dark mountains. *Of home.*

Pulling away, yet taking my hand, I enjoy the way his laughter fills me with light. Warmth spreads as we stride over to the tub where Ardella is bending over it, testing the temperature.

Ro moves to smack her ass, and she yelps before throwing the used towel at him.

Shaking my head, I use the bathroom and return to a filled tub.

We all get in, and Roman leans his back against the porcelain, then me against him, followed by My Lady of Death in my lap.

"This is nice with all of us." She leans into me momentarily as Roman's arms encircle around us. "I like this. It feels so easy," she murmurs to herself, wetting her arms.

"Far easier than life has ever been for us both," I say, kissing her shoulder. Roman places his lips gently on my shoulder in silent agreement.

"I've been so distracted with *Gildus Prick* and this masquerade that I've been avoiding the inevitable," she begins, sighing heavily. "My father and brother are still missing, and I haven't done a single thing. Surely, they would send out a missing lawyer report or something, right?" She reflects her thoughts aloud, rationalizing the harsh truth.

Roman and I don't want to spoil the mood, but if neither of them has sent word back and it's not in the norm to disappear, then they are probably both dead.

Neither of us wants to speak it into existence, but it's a strong possibility.

"I would think so," I tell her quietly, "but regardless of what awaits you outside this hotel room, you aren't alone. You have us on your side, and we won't leave you. We will aid in any way we can."

"I couldn't leave you alone if I tried," Roman admits. Ardella pats him on the leg.

"I know. Of course, you're my *main* stalker." I hear her amusement and feel his chest move in a silent laugh.

"And me? Am I not one, too?" I croon softly in her ear.

She leans to the side to gaze at me, *those yellow eyes and their mischief.*

"You are romantic in every way. It's okay when you do it." She beams, kissing me briefly as Ro reaches to grab her breast.

A giggle squeal slides out of her as she swats at him. "I'm offended," he says in a fake pout.

He wasn't.

"You'll get over it." She shrugs as I place my hand on his thigh.

The heat of the water is relaxing, and I find my eyes closing while fully leaning into Roman with my head on his shoulder.

"I could do this all day," I sigh, slow and deep, letting the blissfulness of the moment settle within my soul.

"Me too," Roman whispers, delicately running his hands through my hair.

It's a gesture that makes me melt further into him.

"Me three," Ardella adds. "We can sit here for a while; the world doesn't need us right at this moment, so why don't we stay on our own?"

She leaned back as we both agreed with her.

"I couldn't agree more. We'll relax and bathe until the water is cold," I tell them both.

We do just that. Exist in the moment. We *needed* it. Our night together happened, and our sinful morning would make all the priests rebuke us.

Our God is a woman, and she would be our death.

E.G.POA

CHAPTER TWENTY-TWO

HERE TO HELP

ARDELLA

"Thank you for coming."

I open the door, revealing my best friend from college. Her midnight hair reminds me of the reaper herself. Silent yet sweet with the promise of torture if deserving.

She hugs me. "I'm here to help. You've been on my mind lately."

Anabel Lee steps over the threshold, taking in the surroundings.

"Your house is creepy, but in a good way... I think?"

Offering a smile, I shrug afterward. A funeral home has a certain ambiance that could only be decorated for *lightness* so much. It didn't change its bones to appear more than what it was. A place for death in *all* aspects.

"Yeah, probably, but look at who you're talking to." I give her an unmistakable look that tricks a smile onto her perfect face.

I missed her so much.

"You still haven't heard anything from your brother or dad?" She asks while I lead her into the kitchen and begin making a soothing herbal tea.

"No, but Roman and Jackson were inquiring around town. They're away in the city now. I told them you were coming, so they felt more comfortable leaving me alone in this house."

"So, you snagged yourself two men now, did you?" Ignoring me when I turn around, her eyebrow is quirked, and my lips stretch wide shamelessly.

While she giggles, I sigh dramatically. "Why choose when I can have them both?"

"Green with envy, Deli."

I huffed a laugh, shaking my head at the ridiculous nickname she came up with while we were drunk at a dorm party one night years ago. Instead of Ardella or Ella, she shortened it to Della but said Deli instead. Somehow, she remembered the next day.

Now, it's a ridiculous inside joke between us. Although I wasn't complaining about our antics, I realized long ago how precious it was to have someone close and loyal. Especially after the heartache from *fucking Rigswold*.

"Alright, Beli," I tease back using my nickname for her in return, "sugar in your tea?"

"You know how I like it," she confirms while the kettle brews.

"I know, *My Little Whore*."

Her laughter echoes while she brings up the college nostalgia of our party nights, and my spirit feels joy over our familiar bantering.

We didn't mean anything by what we said since it was how we talked to each other. Our expression of affection. Also, who cares about other people? *Or what they think.*

"I missed you, My Little Slut," she coos back.

I bump my ass playfully into the side of hers as she winks, and I move around to grab mugs. Anabel stands at the counter waiting as I do.

Moments later, I bring her the sugar added tea, and she breathes it in dramatically.

"This smells amazing, thank you."

"Of course. I missed you too, by the way," I say with a smile, catching her happiness radiating around her.

Turning back around, I fix up my tea, less sweet than hers, and sit next to her, beginning to fill her in about stuff at home and the masquerade.

"At the same time? Damn, that takes me back." She looks off into the distance fondly, no doubt remembering our college shenanigans.

"You inspired me," I wiggle my eyebrows.

"Bitch don't act like we weren't getting fucked in the same room! *Or that you didn't like watching or being watched.*"

It's my turn to burst into laughter with her, nearly choking on my tea.

Before I know it, we're spending the rest of the afternoon over several cups of tea, doubling over in laughter. Just like old times.

"Well, Deli, it sounds like shit has been rough... Before you reached out, I moved back home near the sea where I grew up... *Also,* you *do* know there are telephones, right? You don't have to use the old fashioned way of letters." She inclines her brow before muttering under her breath, *"Even if society delays their non-oppressive views of women..."*

With a shrug of my shoulders, I reply, "I know, but you know me, I don't conform to the world around me."

Scoffing, she sighs in defeat. "True..."

"How is it back at home? Did you run into your childhood lover, too?"

She shakes her head, looking off into the distance. Before I can question her, she answers for me.

"I wasn't back long enough to check... The house was left to me. It needs to be fixed up, but I figured it could wait until after we find out what's going on with you and your family. I'm sorry about Kenzie."

Her face falls when she gives me her empathetic condolences.

Grateful for her friendship during this strange time, and from before, I look down at my hands and whisper, *"Me too."*

She rubs my shoulder. "You won't have to go through it alone, Deli."

I nod, exhaling slowly and completely. The back of my mind keeps whispering that neither my brother nor my father is alive. What will I do if I'm left alone with no blood relatives? Could I survive?

Did I want to?

I refuse to live in this house of ghosts for the rest of my life. Being a mortician isn't bringing me the same joy as it did years ago. I can't fathom how I'd manage Poa's Mortuary Services solo.

My chest aches over my morbid thoughts as I show her to my brother's room. It is plain and boring to my tastes, but he hasn't been there in months. Reynolds was mostly clean and tidy, but he was a damn good legal consultant and lawyer. He also knew medical stuff from growing up here like I did.

She places her bags down near the beige-covered bed. "Now, tell me again about the Masquerade. In *great* detail!"

I grin as I suggest making us some drinks and gossiping some more.

Not admitting it aloud, but her showing up that day kept me from breaking completely.

"I know you have a background in biology, too, but I must say, *Beli*, you are a *natural!*"

I stand on the left side of the forty-year-old male decedent with Anabel next to me on my right. After a couple of weeks, a body was sent over, so some business started up. Because I had medical experience, I was quickly able to figure out lies during the body drop-off. *I had help coming.*

"Hand me that artery tube for this artery, please," I add, distracting my thoughts and indicating the instrument tray.

I adjust my gloves slightly, glad I put the black apron on for the body preparation process Anabel is aiding me with. *My temporary fill in, since no one was available.*

"Here you go." She hands me the tube I ask for as I get to work on inserting the tube in the carotid artery while she finishes up the final touches of the decedent's mouth closure.

Once the tube is set in place, one for fluids going into the carotid artery and one for the blood out of the vein.

I set a two hour timer and double check everything is set. Now, the work continues.

"How can you stand the smell of formaldehyde?" She winces while we begin the process of whole body massaging.

I shrug. "You eventually become nose blind."

Frowning, she sighs. "Of course, you would say that... This process takes two hours, right?"

I give her a nod. "Well, it varies from person to person, but for this decedent, two hours."

Then, she asks me a question I can't begin to answer. "Anything on your brother and father? Did you hear back from your men?"

Focusing on massaging the decedent's head, I shake my head.

"Not a word from authorities?"

With another shake of my head, I carefully massage the face. "What the fuck? What is it with this Morella town? It's so weird and old worldly up here. You have electricity and modern facilities, but the authorities aren't doing shit for missing persons? Did they give up?"

I don't answer while she huffs and puffs in my stead. I had already wracked my brain, coming up as empty-handed as the cops. All I knew was that my father was having financial troubles; how bad it was, I had no clue. It's not like I knew anything about his life outside of the work we did in the basement. The waiting around was driving me insane.

Without Jack and Ro, I would've been eating wallpaper or injecting myself with embalming fluid.

"Stupid follow up question... You truly have no idea where they are?"

"I do not." I move to the opposite side of Anabel, working on the upper extremities. "It's so bizarre and mysterious. No one just *vanishes*. It's all so sketchy, and I have a bad feeling, Beli. I only know of my father's gambling and financial problems and no telling with my brother. Maybe they got mixed up into something terrible?"

We share a knowing look. Dread fills me. There's no way, after all these weeks, they're alive.

Not knowing anything is killing me.

"We'll get through it, either way." She gives me a look of resolve and comfort. "I'm here now, Deli, and I'm not going anywhere until you tell me otherwise. Alright?"

I incline my head, still massaging the skin beneath me. "Thank you. You'll meet the guys tomorrow. They've stayed away these past few days to give us some time together while they do some more digging on their own."

At the mention of digging, I begin to wonder if they still resort to grave robbing to get by in their *profession*.

"Yes, tell me more!"

I stifle a laugh. "Ask away, bitch."

I glance up to see her thinking about it while massaging the decedent's thigh.

"Well, how did you meet?"

My mouth quirks up over the memory of their plan to rob the house.

So, I decided to spill all the morbid details of our wholesome beginning and how I secretly enjoyed Roman and his annoying antics since the beginning. When I get to the library story—*all of the times there*—she gasps.

"*Whatttt*," she draws out for five seconds in surprise.

"It was so fucking hot, Beli." I make a dramatic sound of swooning as she giggles.

"I'm *definitely* jealous. They sound hot... But, do you have room for one more?" She wiggles a brow, teasing me.

"Ask them yourself and see how it goes?"

Anabel grins so big, I would've thought her cheeks filled with *fluid*.

"Don't threaten me with a good time," she answers with sass, and I love her for it.

Rolling my eyes, I tell her the rest about my two stalkers.

"I can't wait until tomorrow." Her excitement is contagious once I finish the story later.

A smirk leaves me. "It'll be nice to see them again after the long week, although I do appreciate your assistance. You're a natural," I compliment. "All of our gossiping has made the time fly. No complaints there, though. Just have to ensure things are tied up, take the cannula and forceps out, and clean up here. Ready?"

She nods, giving me a thumbs up as we finish up with cleaning and giving the decedent the final bath.

Once we're done, Anabel sighs heavily in exhaustion as we leave the basement. "Wanna get drunk and make fun of Prick Furrows?"

"Why, Beli, you do know the love language of this poor unfortunate soul, don't you?"

"Obviously, you morbid bitch. I love you."

I lean my head on hers as we spend the night doing just that.

It makes me feel better knowing my best friend is finally here.

E.G.POA

CHAPTER TWENTY-THREE

FUCK, I'VE MISSED YOU

ARDELLA

"Wow, they're pretty hot."

Their grins stretch from ear to ear when Anabel and I answer the door.

"You two look like you're going to a funeral," Ro says, kissing my cheek as I narrow my eyes.

Well, considering we did...

Jack kisses my other cheek while they step inside the threshold.

The two men take each of Ana's hands, kissing the top.

Then, this drunk bitch says, "You need an extra temporary girlfriend, right?"

I snicker, shaking my head and handing them an empty shot glass each.

"She's four shots deep, don't mind her."

Part of me knew she was serious, and the other part of me doesn't mind; I can tell the two of them don't know what to think, so they neglect to respond.

This will be fun.

Ana is swaying with delight with her rosy cheeks before clumsily pouring all of us a shot.

"Shut up and drink your shot." She hands them all out, and I wink teasingly at her.

"Have you corrupted our Arde?" Ro says after making a face over the burn of the liquor, and I reel in my silent laugh.

"Arde?" She tilts her head curiously. "*Deli* is much better than *Arde*," she says matter-of-factly.

"Deli?" Jack asks slowly with confusion, and Roman is simply smirking, clearly enjoying my friend's sass.

So, I tell them the story, and somehow, it fits the situation at hand. Drunk *again*.

"Good thing we don't live in the big city," Ro begins, and I arch my brow, "or everyone would think you two are extreme lushes."

Ana belts out a laugh. "Oh, like the rest of them aren't? Puh-lease."

I give Ro a look of agreement. "Drunk girl is right." The men shake their heads.

"We are menaces," Ana adds, shooting me a naughty look while pouring more shots. "You didn't answer me before, Roman and Jackson."

The use of their full names makes them stand at attention, and I find it endearing as they stare at her from either side of me. She watches from across the counter before both men side-eye me.

"What was the question?" Roman takes the lead as I turn my head to Jack, giving him my best sneaky smile.

Here it comes.

Instead of answering, she groans, leaning her head on the counter.

My poor best friend—*I'll help you out.*

"Let's show them what we're talking about, Beli. They're confused. And lost. Aren't you?" I probably sound condescending in my low baby-talk voice, but after a few shots myself, I wonder what these men will think of sharing my best friend.

It wouldn't be the first or last time, if they allowed it.

I playfully rub their sides, debating which of them will take to Anabel more; I know they both will, but Roman indirectly volunteers himself.

Ana peeks up directly at me as I grin shamelessly. Taking Jack's hand, I lead him to the couch in the living room that's plenty big for all of us.

"Sit."

He flops down on the right side, gazing up at me under his lashes. I'm already heating up at the sight while I pull up my black dress with a lace collar and climb into his lap, straddling him.

"Ard—" My lips cut him off as I thrust my hand into his locks, reveling in how much I missed him.

I hear his mirrored moan as he interrupts. "Are you sure this is okay?"

"Yes, it is completely okay. Is it alright with you both?" I look at him before shooting my gaze to Ro, who stands on the opposite side of the couch with a certain look in his eyes.

My eyes slowly travel down to where I see a thickening of his cock, indicating to me my answer from him.

"I knew our Arde was special and feisty," Ro answers.

"It's fine by me as long as everyone is comfortable," Jack says immediately afterward before I start grinding in his lap, stealing those precious lips once more.

"I must say, I've had many fantasies, and this wasn't one, but I'm not complaining." Ro sits next to Jack and me as I kiss him hello when he leans in.

I find myself burning up more as their hands begin to wander. Jack's go up my thighs while Roman fists my hair, deepening the kiss.

"And here I thought I was making a bad first impression by this idea," Anabel's voice lingers as she stalks toward Roman.

Ro gives me one last look, his brown gaze delightful and lovely over the situation at hand.

"I think I like you already," he says, turning his face to focus on her.

Ana pulls up her plain black dress and straddles Ro.

"You're like another version of My Little Raven," he places his two fingers under her chin.

"I'll be whoever you want me to be," she says before sealing their lips together.

I smile to myself, seeing Jack's eyes brighten in interest. When I have his eyes on me, I pull off my dress completely, revealing myself bare underneath.

"Fuck, I've missed you," he goes on, taking a breast into his mouth.

I tug on my lip, leaning my head back as his arms go around me, holding me close.

"Follow their lead, big boy," I hear Ana say, and I open my eyes briefly to see her strip bare.

Happy with Ro paying her some attention, I close my eyes again when I feel one hand loosen from around me, squeezing my ass and moving towards my pussy.

"Yes," I whisper, encouraging Jack to continue.

I see a speckle view of colors from his perfect eyes looking up at me.

"My naughty girl."

"*All yours*," I say, sighing blissfully once he circles my clit.

Riding those skillful fingers, I bask in the moans beside me of my other two favorite people and focus on Jack's firm but tender caresses.

"And I missed you," I whimper, feeling the rise of my first orgasm.

"That's it, my angel, just like that," he tucks my nipple between his teeth, stroking my inner walls and thumbing my clit.

"*Fuck,*" I get out as the rise hits, and I tumble down into bliss suddenly, shaking against him.

"Mmm," Jack sounds, pulling me closer to him.

His tongue licks my lip before I open my mouth for him, tasting him while hearing Ana come for Ro.

I unbutton Jack's long-sleeved shirt, exposing his chest. "Your turn, baby," I murmur against his lips, eager to have him in my mouth.

His soft sigh warms my lower belly. I move my lips from his and trace kisses and licks down his jaw and body, inching slowly off his lap and down to the floor.

I see those colors swirling in his eyes, lust prevalent and begging to break free under my touch.

Jack assists me with taking his pants off, and I toss them aside when he's done. I give him a simpering look under my lashes before glancing beside me to see Ana doing the same.

Roman is naked and ready to go.

"Do you two kiss at all?" Ro wonders aloud, and I'm appreciating the sight of the men with their hard, aching cocks, begging for Ana's and my attention.

I see her bite her lip before turning her head while I'm already leaning over to kiss her.

"Well, that answers that, Ro. Come here," Jack says, and we turn our heads to view them kissing.

My heart melts more as I indicate my head to my best

friend. With a quick smile, she leans to take Ro's cock in her mouth, causing a gasp to escape him. Since his eyes are closed and focused on Jackson, he doesn't see it coming.

Ro's eyes flicker to me briefly before focusing on Ana.

"You little minx," he says before I catch Jack observing and biting his lip.

I'm already wet and ready to go again when I follow suit to take Jack's cock into my mouth. It's already leaking with precum as I taste it on my lips. I feel him stiffen underneath before he relaxes, taking a fistful of hair.

"With all these sights and sensations, this won't take long, my love," Jack whispers as I peek up and see his head rearing back, mouth falling open in soft sighs and moans.

"I agree," Ro chirps, reaching for Jack until they're kissing and their tongues are combining.

Closing my eyes, I wrap my hand at his base, focusing my movements on his pleasure. Bobbing my head and adding suction to him, I realize how true his words are when he falls apart and feeds me full of him less than a minute later. His hand tightens in my hair as I swallow him down, moaning loudly so he feels it more intensely with the vibrations.

The sounds he makes cause my eyes to roll to the back of my head, seeing and hearing how I make him come undone. The greatest joy for me, in general, is seeing how they come undone for each other and me; now, it's no different.

I hear Roman moan with his release, and my eyes fall open, releasing Jack from my mouth.

"Fuck me. Are you two in sync or what?" Ro huffs out.

Ana releases him in turn with an innocent smile on her face. "This isn't the first time you two have done this, is it?" Jack questions, and I shake my head.

It certainly isn't, and we take pride in it.

"We were party girls in college and loved to get buzzed and fuck."

Their eyes heat up at Ana's response.

Hiding my sly grin, I stand up with a stretch, moving toward the kitchen.

"One more round of shots?" I ask, seeing Ana follow suit. "You already know I'm here for it, you sexy bitch," Ana says, smacking my ass.

A slight yelp escapes me as I pour more liquor into the shot glasses.

"It won't take the guys long to be ready for more. They're just as insatiable as we are," I tell her as she kisses my cheek with a giggle.

"Good. Shall we switch and give the other some love, too?" I nod in response, handing her the shot glass.

"We're right here, you know. We *can* hear you."

I blow a kiss at Roman when he comes to my side, then he kisses my other cheek and grabs my ass.

"Who said we were trying to hide our intentions?" I ask coyly, and those brown eyes flare up.

"Mmm, My Little Raven, you are asking for a good fucking, aren't you?"

I melt under that stare, handing him his glass. Jackson appears, grabbing his, and all of us clink and drink.

"Yahow!" Ana yells out in victory, and I can't help but laugh.

"You two are something else," Jack careens, amusement on his face before scooping up Ana suddenly.

The delightful sound that leaves her mouth makes me grin. I can see Jack is warming up and delighting in Ana's playfulness. It's sweet to see.

"In the kitchen or elsewhere?" He offers her.

"Well, fuck me, you're giving me options, Jacky boy?" Ana questions.

"See, I like her," Ro adds while I lean into him, fondly observing two of my favorite people in front of me.

Jack keeps his amusement in his voice. "Never mind, to the couch with you."

She giggles before he kisses her, dropping her onto the couch while continuing to kiss her.

Swooning over the scene, I turn to Ro.

"I missed you too, love," I tell him, wrapping my arms around him to meet his luscious lips.

He groans, picking me up and setting me on the countertop. That glorious cock prods at my entrance as he stands between my legs.

"I wasn't expecting this today, but you continue to surprise me, My Little Raven."

I run my hands up his chiseled chest and around his back, appreciating the strength of the man before me. His smart mouth, the cockiness, *what was between my thighs—all of it.* What began as a mystery and painful undertones of his past became *this* wholesome being in front of me.

"I love you, Roman." I kiss him sweetly and feel him melt under my touch, leaning into me.

"I love you, Ardella."

Dissolving into mist over him using my name, *finally,* instead of his little nickname. I wrap my legs around his waist.

"Now, fuck me hard on this counter, Ro, and make me see stars."

I hear moans from the living room, and both Ro and I turn to see the delicious view of Anabel getting fucked from behind as she grips the back of the couch.

"I can do that, little raven, let me taste that little pussy first."

He kneels and keeps his head wrapped between my thighs before his tongue descends upon me ruthlessly.

I twitch at his assault, gripping the edge of the counter and the edge of the sink with my other hand.

A *fuck* leaves my lips until I jolt at a surprising and quick release, moaning violently and hard.

My head is already swimming when he stands and plows inside me.

"You said to make you see stars, my love... *I intend to*," he says, stretching me at his entry.

"Don't. Stop," I tell him between fast pumps, his hands drifting to my shoulders to hold me in place as he fucks me hard and fast.

My tits bounce as I nearly arch my back entirely off the counter, meeting him thrust for thrust.

"I've missed that tight little pussy of yours, all mine for the taking." He licks his lips; my eyes flutter open and close, feeling the rise of another orgasm riding a wave right toward me.

"Ro," I begin before I'm cut off by a cry, my mouth falling open until I'm spiraling and seeing stars.

"That's my good little raven," he breathes, grunting over how I tighten around him while scooping me up to place me on another counter with the cabinets above.

Roman's lips claim mine, arms closing in around me as I do the same with muffles of moans from us both.

My head is pinned to the cabinet while he devours me. I'm a mess, soaking and not left for wanting. He fulfills my needs and brings me to newer heights. A part of my soul that I share with Jackson.

Love and lust with the two men I cherish most; a world without them is no world at all.

The banter and passion between Roman and I bleed as we tumble off the edge together, crying out in a song made for one another. With my hands in his hair and the feel of him seeping into me, there is nothing but that shared bliss, the shared ecstasy.

A dream within my dream, nothing is unseen. My soul is bare, held together by both men.

There is nothing else for me but them.

E . G . POA

CHAPTER TWENTY-FOUR

I AM DONE

ARDELLA

The burdens have finally caught up.

My father is dead.

The only person in this fucking family who understood me and let me be authentically me. The male who wiped my tears when Rigs left a hole in my heart. The one who supported my dreams, who wanted more for me in life than the funeral home. He never judged, only loving me. The steadfast love of a parent to their child. Teaching me not to fear death but to care for it and find wonder and beauty in it—like with most things in life.

"Death is to be respected. It is not peaceful for everyone, and sometimes the pain lingers for those left behind, but it is not something to fear, Ella. Is it the end of the cycle of life, or is it? None of us know until it's our time, and sometimes we don't know. The unknown can be scary for many, but it holds wonder and truth. A sense of peace if you lived your life or regret if you didn't. None of us know what comes after the brain dies. We know what happens physically, but where does our soul go?

Does it linger and soar, or is there purgatory somewhere for souls who are not damned but not worthy of heaven? All are valid questions of existence, Ella, but always remember that living your life to the fullest is better than none lived at all."

I listened to his wise words as he cleaned endless bodies and showed me the ropes. The care of the dead—*the decedent*—is deserved, especially the ones who lived a hard or lonely life.

"You can always tell what kind of life someone lived by how they arrived. Permanent scars that tell a story, or if there's violence, then they were involved in unfortunate things; sometimes there's nothing wrong, and they come to us from drifting away or old age. No matter their story, my dear, always respect them. Some spirits linger if you aren't careful. I've always feared otherwise if great care wasn't implemented in death care. Sometimes, people don't get the love and care in their life, so they must receive it here. No matter what."

I wipe my wet cheeks as our memories flash before my eyes. Will you linger now, Dad?

Is this all there is now?

Will I meet you in purgatory or an afterlife of some sort?

Feeling the pain too deep, I feel the walls closing in, my lungs with it as my breathing becomes shorter, and then begins the hyperventilation.

It takes me a minute to realize that multiple arms are wrapped around me. I'm being held from all sides.

I'm so out of it, locked in myself, I assume it's my three favorite people.

All I can do is cry.

My brother is still missing, probably indefinitely or dead as well. I can only assume the worst at this point. Especially after a newspaper article saying his law practice went under and he mysteriously disappeared.

There is no family left.

My wails eventually turn to soft cries, then silent ones. Until the well dries up, and all I can do is stare off into space.

I'm uncertain when Anabel finally leaves during my grief, but Jackson and Roman stay.

Anabel had an emergency at home, according to Roman, and he handed me a scribbled note.

> Ardella,
>
> I'm sorry to have to leave you; I received a strange letter and had to return home. Something is amiss, and I will find out the answers. I love you to death, and I will write when I can. Roman and Jackson love you eternally, keep them close.
>
> I'm so sorry about your father, I know how much he meant to you and shaped you into the morbid, lovely woman that you are.
>
> I'm nervous about what I'm returning to, but my heart is with you always.
>
> Until we meet again, Deli. Love Always,
> A. Lee.

I sigh and hope the best for Anabel Lee, for she deserved, 'a love that was more than love'. I will miss her, that's for sure.

Jack and Ro take turns wordlessly bathing or feeding me.

I'm incapable of taking care of myself. They mention, at one point, something about moving my stuff into their place, but I say nothing. I don't particularly care where I live or where I die.

All that is left is dust from the crematorium and silent ghosts of my family tree wandering aimlessly around me.

After the funeral passes by in a blur, I lock myself in my father's room and lay on his sheets, smelling and missing him, along with the fond memories from my youth.

Is it days or weeks at this point?

My only comfort is that his scent still lingers, somehow making me feel closer to him. A small hope that his ghost will haunt me—*the only one I'd wish for.*

It doesn't happen, of course.

The only ghost in this house is me.

The sun and moon blend together. I began to wonder if that's how my mother felt about the life she lived, or maybe she didn't feel like she lived at all. It's a relationship I would never know. It's probably a sin to grieve one parent more than the other, but I realize that while people live and breathe, some of them are dead inside before it ever greets their door.

I'm sure weeks passed, or maybe it was days or hours.

Time doesn't answer to grief.

The distance grows, and the emptiness of those who are no longer there.

The only choice is to feel it and let it overcome, dragging and pulling to the bottom of the ocean. Drowning in my self-made misery made of life and death.

When my mother died, I couldn't feel it. When my sister passed, I felt regret that I couldn't do more or be a better sister who stuck around for people. My father died, and it broke me completely. Undone, as if I am in the casket preparing for my eternal sleep.

I'm not sure when I come out of my silent fog, but I'm alone in the house. My room's empty, and as the only haunted ghost in the house, I linger through the walls. Every room. Every floor.

Memories come as whispers in my mind of what was, is, and will never be.

I am done.

I find some gas cans in the shed outside near the crematorium. Part of me debates if I want to set myself on fire. Not sure why I don't, but I came up with a better plan.

I'm going to set this fucking house on fire.

As if the epiphany awakens my mental slumber, I rage through the rooms, throwing shit left and right.

The stages of grief. All erupting out of order. My denial and depression came after the bargaining. Now, I'm dealing with anger. God only knows when the acceptance will hit.

The curse of my family, all dead. All with secrets I'd never know or discover. Perhaps it wasn't my place to know, and I'd eventually have to accept the unknown.

I laughed. I wept. I screamed, and I fought that house with every breath. The heartbeats echoed under the floorboards along with the madness since the house was born into my family.

No more.

Grabbing my father's matches, I walk outside to the front, lighting a cigarette after letting the gasoline trickle off near my feet. I kick off my shoes and throw them on the front porch. Then, I strip naked.

We're born naked, so it was only fair to die naked.

After this, I will bathe in my favorite spot one last time. My long black coat lay some yards away, as I could care less about the chilly night air.

This house was once everything to me; now, it holds nothing for me anymore. I can't live here and will give myself this cathartic moment. I will not touch another body. The old me is dead. There will be no more body preparation, no services, no death; at least, in the way I'm used to.

Now, it's time for it to go up in flames. The only time I'll incinerate this corpse of a house.

It doesn't matter who I'll be after this moment. I no longer care anymore about expectations.

Perhaps E.G. Poa would linger, or maybe she'd do something else entirely from her madness.

I take a puff, letting the match flick onto the trail of gasoline.

I couldn't understand why people liked these cancer sticks; I suppose they looked cool to smell like it and have the aesthetic of smoke in my face, being mysterious and trendy. I stare at it as the house lights up like a goddamn burning Christmas tree. Admiring my handy work, I smile and wipe the tears that sneak out of my eye sockets.

The sight is extraordinary, *hot,* and beautiful. A symbol of my life. It's up in flames, and now it's dead too.

Not knowing how long I stood there, I still hold my great internal debate on going inside the crumbling place and burning with it to complete the family legacy.

Still never figured out why I didn't.

A small part of me that lay hidden under the rubble remembered that two men and possibly my best friend needed me. I still couldn't remember why or when she left. Something must've come up, but I was a shell, locked away in this burning house.

I sigh and flick away the last of the cigarette, coughing slightly before turning my back to focus on the feel of the earth beneath my feet. It doesn't take me too long to make it to my spot with my coat, in the grand scheme of things.

The water is freezing cold, but I don't care. It's better to feel something than nothing at all. I'm merely a living corpse.

I battle my suicidal thoughts as I hold my breath underwater, recognizing that I'm not alone.

I'm not cursed. Just *really* fucking unlucky. My woes were a series of unfortunate happenings, morbidly so. When I'm ready, I'll write about it.

The sky eventually grows brighter, and I shakily make my way to their house...*ours now, I suppose.*

When I show up, they both curse, enveloping me in their arms immediately.

"You're turning blue, Arde, for fuck's sake!"

"We thought you were in that burning house. Don't ever scare us like that again!"

I say nothing as my teeth clatter together, my body shaking hard.

"I'm not even going to ask why you're naked under this damp coat and no shoes... Are you trying to die too?" It's Roman who speaks.

He takes my face into his hands, forcing me to *face him*.

"I thought about it, but I didn't... Wasn't it a masterpiece?"

He chokes out, "You...haven't spoken in weeks. Fuck me, it's so good to hear your voice."

Holding me tight in his arms. I feel Jackson doing the same behind me.

"I'm so sorry," I whisper, crying again, realizing that I shut down completely on them, yet they still remained and gave me space when needed.

"Let's warm you up, Ardella."

Jack scoops me up and takes me to his room. Roman grabs more blankets.

He takes off the coat and tucks me into the center of the

bed. After they situate their blankets around me, they climb in naked, holding me between them.

"We don't have to leave this bed or do anything other than hold you and warm you up. We will figure the future out and get through it," Jack says from behind me, his warmth radiating to my cold, dead heart.

They whisper how much they love me, and eventually, my teeth stop clattering. It will be their warmth that revives me again.

MY REQUIEM

I gaze up at the night sky. The night is clear, with no lights, only stars. Blackness. Vast and endless. I ponder those corpses of the past, long dead now. There, they shine still for lifetimes. Beauty and splendor. Chaos and dreams. Made of the elements, it flows through me.

Someday, will I be like them, too? Will I shine, or will I burn out? Will I be recycled back into the universe?

Do we live on after this life? Will this be it? Resurrection or atonement.

Flames or light, like the stars. It could be purgatory, the dark matter surrounding the galaxies.

Transport me to another world. Let me make it right. The errors and mistakes, longings and regrets. Let me paint the space between the pages, better images, better words. Time before dust and long before they fade.

Let me reconcile or say goodbye. Do the things I've never done and live better than this life gave.

Maybe I'll be more religious, try harder, pray to the saints, or linger in the dark. Or the paganism of the universal truths of nature.

Thoughts lay within the lies of good and evil.

The construct and how society shames—how can we make the world a better place for those deemed unsavable? Is it a lie, too, and we're all damned in the end? What if there wasn't any belief? If I believe nothing, do I become nothing? The space that fills the stars, the veins, and the heart? Where the shadow lingers and cold lies?

Does The Creator hold extraordinary worlds that involve peace and all the things of dreams? A place to hold not the sinner or saint but peace within souls.

Is there a spot for the inbetween?

All I crave is the peace that isn't in vain. To dream and create, explore, and feel free. Without death, without the stains. Without the battle of good and evil. *The battle of me.*

Freedom of the soul, no pain. Love and nature, beauty, art, and music. Endless libraries of fantasies and masterpieces.

The conundrum lies in inspiration. Could such a place exist without the balance of yin and yang? Isn't the whole purpose all about balance? If the scales tip, then corrections must be made.

Why does this have to be? The end feels looming, and life is pain and suffering. Suffer to live, and there's a reward.

It complicates matters of the heart. These questions are without sensical answers. What Creator would create such chaos?

Where is the happy ending to my story, whether this life or the after?

To envision a little dream that isn't all for nothing. Not when I stare up at the view before me. Dark and light coexist in something beautiful upon my naked eye.

The soulmate of two stars colliding, collapsing under pressure, and leaving behind a picture, a moment in the grand scheme of time.

Time rewinds and quickens. All in these memories.

Your memories.

So, take this piece of me, let it drift into the wind.

We have to believe in some sort of final destination. A reason to make it all worth it, a meaning even if none is required. Why would these anatomical particles create these thoughts if for nothing? Oxygen in cells, blood pumping this heart, formal thought, and the lover's kiss.

Whether death embraces me today or tomorrow, It is not for nothing, and this is my requiem.

— E.G. Poa

E.G.POA

EPILOGUE

ARDELLA

We stand on the hill overlooking the town of Morella. The town in the mountains, hidden from the rest of the world. A bittersweet moment of my youth and the ending of the present.

After I leave this place, it will begin anew.

It would no longer be the place between worlds in my mind.

The death place.

I am free of my ghosts and lay them to rest just as I metaphorically laid myself upon those burning flames of my childhood home.

That crime was my own, a freak accident that left the authorities puzzled once I disappeared.

I hid myself away, healing and growing; *writing.*

Let the world think I'm dead, too, for she is.

E.G. Poa will still linger amidst the pages, appearing and disappearing whenever to keep them guessing and wondering where the writer is.

Sometimes, with endings, they end. Or begin. Who's to say what happens?

There lie questions without answers, the unknown, that people fear or shy away from. Those dark corners of the soul that people let rot away under the floorboards of their youth.

A hand on my shoulder brings me back to the *now*.

Now, it's time to leave and begin. "Are you ready?"

Another hand on my side brings my attention to their brown and earthly eyes.

"Yes. Let's finally leave this place," I tell them.

The corners of their mouths lift as they stand beside me and look off below at the town that'll never grow. Their arms circle me, holding me there.

"This will be good for all of us."

I nod my head at Jackson's words of wisdom, part of my binary star in my dark universe.

"No matter what happens after this moment, we have each other."

I lean into Roman's side, appreciating the genetic makeup he is, because he holds the burning binary stars together. *Gravity* holding them close together.

Three parts, working together, colliding or exploding when it's their time to end.

For now, we'll let it burn.

THE END

ACKNOWLEDGMENTS

Hello Preylings.

I hope you enjoyed this standalone *Poe* project!

The inspiration came to me after hearing stories of funeral directing from one of my dearest friends.

Alas, this baby was born. This was a fun story to work on, and I loved experimenting with such new ideas.

Anyway, onto the praises.

Let's start with my beta readers and ARC readers!

To those who have been with me and for all the new readers! I couldn't do this without you! *Along with helping me with my repetitious repetition—*See what I did there? I'm so grateful for the work that goes into being a beta reader! You make me a better writer! *Seriously!* For the ARC readers, *my cheerleaders,* I also can't do any of this without you!

To Colby, you are my fucking rockstar! As you said to me, *"you beautiful bitch."* Your comments and insight have been helpful, and I couldn't do anything without YOU! To the edits, formatting, and everything inbetween. You helped me bring this book to life! I love your face!

Last but certainly not least, to *you,* the reader! No matter how you came across this read, thank you! I'm so happy you stuck around!

Also, spoilers, *Ana* is getting her own standalone book.

Xoxo

R.N. Arcadia

ABOUT THE AUTHOR

R.N. Arcadia is a neurodivergent, day-dreaming Pisces. They live in New Jersey with her family.

When R.N. isn't writing or working, they enjoy traveling, going to the beach, binge-watching/binge-reading whatever series they finds themselves engrossed in, and listening to all sorts of music to stay sane.

https://linktr.ee/r.n.arcadia

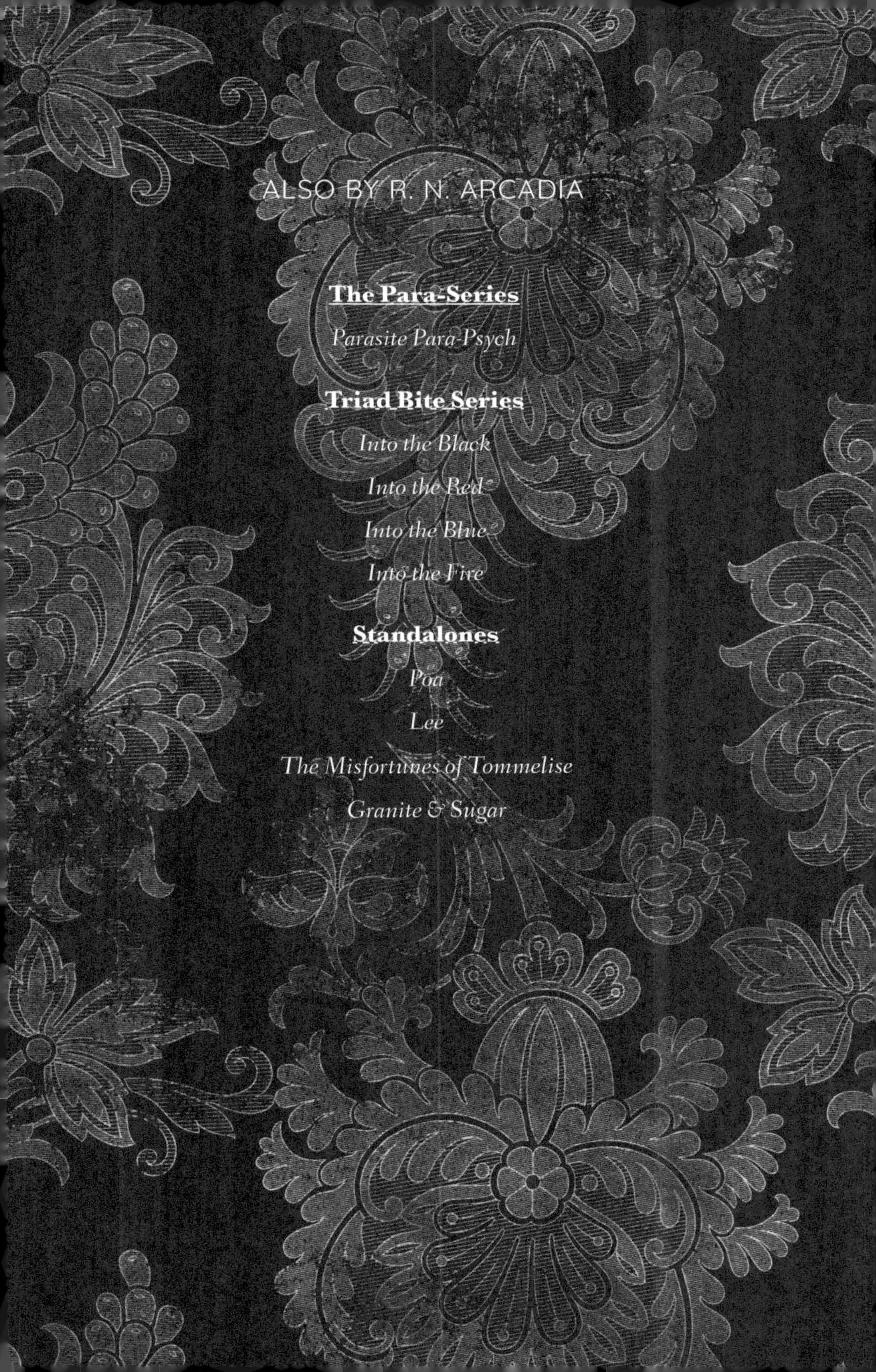

ALSO BY R. N. ARCADIA

The Para-Series
Parasite Para-Psych

Triad Bite Series
Into the Black
Into the Red
Into the Blue
Into the Fire

Standalones
Poa
Lee
The Misfortunes of Tommelise
Granite & Sugar

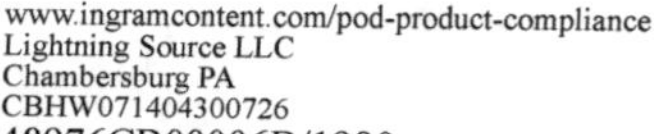
9 798999 984937